Sweet an[...]

By
Anthony Milligan

Copyright © A Milligan

The Moral right of Anthony Milligan to be identified as the author of this work has been asserted in accordance with the Copyright, Design and Patents Act of 1988.

All rights reserved. No part of this work shall be used, copied or stored in a retrieval system, transmitted by any means or photocopied in any form without the written permission of the author or his agents.

Blocat Publications Oldham UK

Foreword

Anthony Milligan has produced a collection of entertaining short stories some serious some comedic. He has divided the book into two parts for ease of the reader. Enjoy.

The Con Artist

Jonas Flint smiled beatifically as he assessed his latest victim across her coffee table. 'What a beautiful home you have Mrs Triton and in such a stunning location, too.'

Rubie Triton glowed, 'why, thank you, Mr Flint, my late husband and I bought it in 1965. It's handy for church and we love the view of the sea, the windmill and the old lifeboat station.' Rubie spent the next ten minutes regaling her visitor with some local history of Lytham-Saint-Anne's. He was impatient to press on, though he never showed it. He would reel her in gently.

He gave a broad, well-practised smile, 'please, would you call me Jonas, Mrs Triton, and may I call you Rubie? So much friendlier, don't you agree?'

'Oh, yes, yes, Jonas, quite.'

Rubie nervously flicked a non-existent crumb from her frumpy twin set and pushed her knitting further away. Her blue-rinsed silver hair was perched above her unworldly face; her watery blue eyes peered out over wire-framed spectacles. Beside her, a cat curled on a well-thumbed puzzle book.

Flint opened his laptop then produced a glossy brochure. 'Learning about your local history is fascinating, Rubie, but I suppose we'd better press on.'

Rubie clasped her hands before her and leaned forward. 'Oh, yes, please do, Jonas, this is so exciting.'

'The Brazilian project I outlined on the phone, Rubie, is a new but simple concept. The population of Brazil is growing exponentially, and their government is hard-pressed to house them, so they are seeking outside investors.'

'I see, and that's where your company comes in.'

'Yes, we've bought a large tract of land to the east of the town of Santos where we intend to build investment properties.' He opened the brochure with a flourish and showed her the neat properties. He omitted to tell her the land was a useless swamp and the small print near the bottom of page six said she was buying land only.

'The properties will be rented to provide funds to pay you a monthly income, Rubie.'

'Oh, that's good, Jonas, my husband's final years in the care home took almost all our savings.'

Flint allowed his mouth to droop, his eyes looking sad. Adopting a carefully rehearsed sincere tone, he said 'that is why I proposed this scheme, Rubie, I believe it answers all your requirements. Our investors supply the capital to build, and the Brazilian Government guarantee the rents, so we can pay you one per cent per month on your investment. In your case, three hundred thousand will pay you three thousand pounds per month, after the first year, of course.' He produced some impressive looking documents. 'This is the statement of guarantee for the rents from the Brazilian government and this is the English translation.' He laid the flawlessly forged documents before her with the air of a man presenting a diamond necklace. 'These and your deeds of ownership will be sent to you should you decide to take advantage of this opportunity, Rubie.'

Rubie's eyes opened a little wider and she reached for the lengthy documents her fingers caressing them. Then a hesitant smile flickered across her face. 'But can I withdraw part of my money in the future, Jonas? I have twin grandsons, fatherless since my poor son passed away. I want to put them through university, you see. I'll need about sixty thousand pounds in three years.'

Flint oozed reassurance 'of course, Rubie, you may sell all or part of your investment either privately or to us. We guarantee to repurchase at the market price less three per cent.'

'Oh, that's marvellous, Jonas.' A tear formed in the corner of her eye, and she sniffed, dabbing with a lace handkerchief. 'I may appear to be a prosperous widow, but this money is the very last of my savings.'

Flint made a sympathetic moué, 'then it's lucky you found us, Rubie, this is the last sub-tract to be sold. You're only just in time.'

Sweet and Sour

'Oh!' Rubie's eyebrows shot up 'Oh, do I have to make my mind up right away, Jonas?'

'Gracious me, no, Rubie. Please take all the time you require. However, I do have other appointments today and once this opportunity is gone it's gone forever, I'm afraid.'

Rubie hesitated, wringing her hands, indecision writ large on her face 'you know, Jonas, my husband used to say, "never rush into things, always do business in a business-like manner."'

'Sound advice, Rubie.'

'Do you have a copy of your company's accounts I could see, Jonas?'

'I'm afraid the company accounts are held in Brazil, Rubie, and written in Portuguese.'

'Surely your company have a bank account in this country, Jonas? Perhaps you could show me the balance? One hears so many dreadful tales these days and this investment is crucial for the future of my dear grandsons and me.'

Flint smiled obsequiously, 'but of course, Rubie.' His fingers rattled the computer keys then he turned the screen to face her. There you are, but it's only the local operating funds I'm afraid.'

Rubie peered over her rims 'one million seven hundred and… oh, I'm so sorry I doubted you, Jonas, but it is vital to me.' She stood up suddenly 'come along, dear Jonas' she said firmly 'I always walk before making important decisions.' He quickly logged out of the banking page and followed her to the front door.

They strolled across The Green to the windmill, her enthusiasm for local history resurfacing. 'Such a beautiful old mill, Jonas. It has quite a chequered history since it was built around 1805. It burnt out in 1919 then the owner, Squire, John Clifton of Lytham Hall, gave it to the town. Since then, it's been a café, a storeroom and even an electricity sub-station. It was an eyesore before the council rescued it. Now we have a lovely museum along with the old lifeboat station there. Quite the tourist attractions these days.'

Flint forced a smile; the longer this took the less likely she was to take the bait. He was impatient to conclude his nefarious business and be gone. 'So interesting, Rubie' he simpered 'no wonder you love living here, but about the investment…'

Rubie clapped her hands together in a prayer position, her eyebrows arching. 'Oh, my apologies, Jonas, I do prattle on, let's go back at once and do the paperwork. My mind is quite made up.'

Papers signed; Flint required payment. 'I'll give you our bank details Rubie so that you can transfer the funds now.' He spun the laptop towards her.

Rubie recoiled, throwing her hands up. 'Goodness me, Jonas, I don't use those infernal computer things. I'll write you a cheque, my dear.' She dived into her handbag.

Sweet and Sour

Flint felt alarmed until he saw her chequebook. 'Ah, Coutts, you bank with the Queen's bankers.' He perked up, he knew it took a minimum of half a million pounds to open an account with Coutts Bank. He glanced at the French mantle clock, he still had time to make the bank and special-clear the cheque. The cash would be his by tomorrow. Flint quickly concluded his sting and departed his heart rejoicing.

*

Fifty-five-year-old Elsa Tweedy sat in the conservatory of the Lakeside Hotel in Ambleside watching the swans gracefully mugging the tourists for tidbits. 'Ah, there you are Aunt Elsa, that was *so* exciting.'

The two women embraced affectionately 'Success was due in no small measure to you, Louise, thanks to your expertise as a make-up artist. That blue rinse wig, the wire-rimmed spectacles, and that god-awful twin set.' She laughed joyfully 'I certainly did look like a doddery old biddy. You did *so* well.'

'Oh, but my bit was easy, Aunt. When you left, with Flint, I came downstairs, retrieved the hidden camera, and got his bank details and password. I simply transferred all his ill-gotten gains into your Swiss numbered account.'

They laughed again, then Louise became serious 'Well, you certainly got all my mother's money back from that horrid man and a nice bonus for yourself, too.'

'A bonus for us, dear Louise, for us.'

Louise's brow furrowed as she wrinkled her nose. 'So, how did you acquire access to that beautiful house and a Coutts cheque book?'

Elsa leaned back in her chair, her eyes sparkling, 'I answered an advertisement for a house sitter, my dear.' She blushed, breaking eye contact. 'As for the cheque book?' a forgery, I'm afraid. I have friends in extremely low places.' Then she quickly brightened, 'by the way, did you like the name I chose?'

'Rubie Triton? Yes, an anagram of retribution, you and your puzzles, Elsa.' She grinned 'I wonder if Flint will work it out?'

'I do hope so.'

'But your numbered Swiss account, Elsa, that's real and no one in the family even suspected you had one.' Her brow creased again above her narrowed eyes. 'Come to think of it, Aunt, none of us knows what you actually do for a living. I mean, the title "Businesswoman" covers a multitude of sins.'

Elsa smiled mischievously 'a great multitude in my case, dear niece.' She winked and tapped the side of her nose, 'but some things are best left secret, my dear. Now, shall we order lunch?'

The Pendle Pilgrim

'How many times, George, do I have to say it? There are no such things as ghosts.' A sharp breath exploded through Hilda's lips, and she shook her head in exasperation. 'Your surname may be Device, but that is not evidence that you are a descendant of the Pendle witches. Witches, for God's sake! Really, George, in this day and age?'

George's head bowed and his face flushed, his eyes unable to meet hers, his spirit desolate. How could he make her understand?

George didn't want to accompany Hilda to the ruins of the ancient house that recent digging for a new electricity line had uncovered. His voice trembled, 'they discovered a mummified cat in the wall, Hilda, proving witchcraft was practised there all those years ago.' He spread his hands, pleading, his eyes wide. 'I know their presence still lurks in such places, Hilda, I feel it.' He loved his wife dearly and these arguments distressed him deeply.

'I want to go and see the place, George,' she insisted, 'you know my interest in local history, you're just being selfish, letting childish fears get the better of you.'

'United Utilities can dig up a whole village, Hilda, and I still wouldn't go to look. Every time I get close to that hill, I feel them near me, their sorrow drowns me in misery.'

Hilda's eyes narrowed like gun slits, as the dominant partner in their marriage, she hated being thwarted. Her voice rose angrily. 'Even if your ancestors do haunt Pendle Hill, it's because they were evil people and richly deserved their fate.' Hilda snatched her car keys from the table. She would visit the ancient house without him. That what she regarded as superstitious nonsense still lingered in people like her husband annoyed her intensely. 'It's history, not mystery, George. Sod you, I'm off.'

*

When Hilda arrived, the ancient house was deserted. The plastic tape which had surrounded it with a "Danger do not cross" warning was now tattered and streaming forlornly in the wind like the remnants of ancient heraldic banners.

The ruins were not large, but they had an eerie atmosphere. Her knowledge of ancient architecture was limited to castles, her knowledge of common dwellings was sketchy at best. This visit would improve it.

As Hilda examined the wall where they had found the mummified cat, she was overcome with tiredness.

Sweet and Sour

Arguing with George always exhausted her. She sat on a large stone by the hearth and crossed her arms about her shoulders rubbing vigorously against the suddenly chilly air. She wondered why the sky had darkened.

'Welcome to my house missus.'

Startled, Hilda looked up. The woman, clad in a long grey dress, was barely discernible against the grey stones of the wall. She was ugly, one of her eyes was lower than the other, and a couple of warts grew from her nose giving her a malevolent look. Hilda's soul froze. 'Who…. who are you?'

'My name is, or was, Elizabeth Device, Hilda, an ancestor of your George, one of the souls you say deserved to die so unjustly.'

Hilda's voice quavered 'I…I don't believe in you.' she squeezed her eyes tightly shut hoping the apparition would disappear.

'Don't care what you believe my lady, I'll show you my truth. You shall come upon a pilgrimage of pain with me.'

Hilda's head spun, she felt she was in a dream, yet was not. Her whole being trembled, 'OK,' she said, 'this is a hoax set up by my husband. I'm leaving now.'

'That you are missus. You're coming with me to Lancaster gaol. You'll see what I saw, feel what I felt, then tell me if I deserved such a cruel fate.'

Hilda found herself being drawn from her body towards the apparition and then into the woman's body. She screamed in horror, helpless as her soul was absorbed.

'Scream as loud as yer like Missus, none will hear you.'

Then Hilda was laying in the back of a farm cart its fixed axles bumping painfully over a rough track. All her senses felt heightened. The creak of the harness was loud in her ears and the smell of horses was strong in her nostrils. The sky was unnaturally bright.

There were others in the cart, including a young girl. 'That's my daughter Jennet she is but nine years old.' It was Elizabeth's voice she heard in her head.

The cart bumped on all day the only stops were for the horses to drink. No water was offered to them. They stopped for the night near the village of Whalley where they were thrown into a barn, men standing guard over them.

One of the guards came over to Elizabeth. Hilda. could smell his unwashed body and foul breath. 'Give me that ring, witch.' He tugged at her little finger until it almost broke, but the little gold ring didn't move.

'This ring has been on my finger since girlhood, good sir. It doesn't come off,' said Elizabeth.

The guard drew his knife. 'Oh, don't it, witch?' he scoffed, 'we'll see about that.'

Sweet and Sour

Hilda felt a wave of terror flood her Oh, please God, no, she thought as she felt the man grip her finger spreading it. Elizabeth screamed as the knife bit.

'Don't you be cutting off her damned finger Samuel Blotch' the voice was harsh and commanding 'she'll be wailing all night and we'll never get any sleep.' It was the headman of the party. 'She'll be hung soon enough, do it then.'

Reluctantly, the man released her and went away muttering 'tis my ring, I claimed it first.'

After another long day's travel, bumping over rough roads and being jeered at by the people of the villages they passed through, they arrived at Lancaster gaol. The cart trundled in, and Hilda found herself thrown into a dark damp cell. Jennet was dragged away screaming for her mother. Hilda felt Elizabeth's despair, her pain of separation that only a mother could know.

There was a little damp straw on the floor to offer scant comfort and a bucket in the corner. The night was long, cold and sleepless. When the dawn came, they were given stale bread and water. Later, Elizabeth was dragged in chains into the courtroom where the magistrate glowered balefully.

'This is wrong' Hilda screamed. 'Elizabeth, please, release me.' She got no response.

'Elizabeth Device you are charged with murdering John and James Robinson by witchcraft and consulting with the devil. How plead ye?'

'Not guilty, sir.'

'Not guilty? But we have a witness, woman.'

'I have killed no one, sir.'

'Bring forth the witness.'

Jennet was brought in, her left hand now in a crude bandage, her eyes red-rimmed with tears. She looked around her fearfully. They stood her on a footstool in the centre of the room, all eyes boring into her.

'Jennet Device do ye bear witness against this woman?' the magistrate rasped. Jennet looked down trembling and nodded.

'Speak, girl, lest thou share her fate.'

'Yes, sire.'

'No,' screamed Elizabeth 'this cannot be allowed, my daughter is but a child.'

Jennet was made to tell a tale of how she'd seen her mother consulting her familiar, a black dog. Of how she saw her make clay images and cursed them, causing the brothers Robinson to die.

Elizabeth screamed at her daughter 'Tell the truth Jennet, please my darling.' Hilda felt every stab of her pain and despair wash through her. She was dragged from the court in hysterics; they proceeded without her.

Sweet and Sour

Hilda felt Elizabeth slowly becoming calm, resigned now to her fate. She was dragged back into court and the verdict of guilty was announced. She was sentenced to death by hanging.

'After you have murdered me, sir, she told the magistrate, 'I shall return in spirit to my beloved house in the forest of Pendle. Lay my bones where you will and be damned to you.'

Hilda felt terrified; she didn't want to share Elizabeth's fate; the injustice was soul-shattering. She screamed in her terror. 'Be calm my lady, death is nought to fear.' Elizabeth told her.

Next day Elizabeth was led to the scaffold. She walked calmly looking the sneering hangman in the eye. 'For your sins, shall ye die screaming' she told him. 'A cancer in thy bowels.' She spat at his feet and derived great satisfaction from seeing his sneer fade, replaced by fear in his eyes.

Hilda felt rough hands bind her wrists, the coarse rope chaffing. She was lifted onto a stool. Below her was a mob baying for blood. Some were laughing and joking others hurling insults. A few looked on fearfully, their hands clasped in prayer. A priest stood off to one side, his eyes fixed on a prayer book as he mumbled.

The noose scratched her neck as it tightened, 'No, please, Elizabeth, let me go, please' Hilda screamed.

'Death will release us both, Hilda.'

The stool was kicked away without ceremony and the rope jerked tight. Hilda felt herself being strangled, her feet kicking wildly. Then, as the rope closed more tightly, the blood supply to her head was cut off and she rapidly lost consciousness.

*

Hilda woke with a start and let out a yelp of fear and surprise to find herself back in the ruined house. She sat up, confused, her hand rubbed her neck, it was painless. Slowly she recovered her faculties. A dream, she told herself, just a vivid dream. That's what comes of listening to George. But it was twenty minutes before she could drive home.

Back home, she told her tale to George 'I tell you, George, the dream was so real, so terrifying...'

'It was no dream' said George sombrely 'it was a visitation.'

'A visitation?' She laughed nervously, 'you know, George, I could almost believe you.'

George pointed to her little finger 'Tell me, then, Hilda, where did you get that ring?'

Hilda looked down at her hand, screamed, then fainted.

A Change of Heart

I was thirteen before I realised what an utterly selfish, attention-seeking woman my mother was. Father was her opposite, a gentle, mild-mannered soul who avoided all confrontation. If mother was opposed, she had a 'funny turn,' and dad would acquiesce.

In my youth, we spent Christmas at Grandma's 200 miles away in Lincoln. On our final visit, grandma greeted us lovingly then mother pulled her usual stunt 'I'll have to rest Reginald' she whined, 'my headaches so.' She quickly disappeared upstairs leaving dad and me to help grandma with the preparations. Mother reappeared when the arduous work was done, then commandeered grandma's armchair and the TV remote. She channel-hopped, complaining loudly about the rubbish they put on at Christmas.

Dad saw my irritation and mouthed, 'shush, Elizabeth, she'll have a turn.' Then grandma called us to dinner, thank God.

'I'll just nip to the loo.' mother said.

We sat; minutes ticked by Grandma called upstairs 'Are you all right, Cynthia?'

'Yes, dear.'

After another five minutes Grandma sighed 'Elizabeth, dear, would you please go and check on your mother?'

Mother was mirror-gazing leisurely applying makeup. 'I'll be down in a minute' she snapped.

Eventually, she appeared, beaming a crocodilian smile and sitting down without a word of apology. We ate our now congealing dinner in silence. The meal over, mother crassly quipped 'that was a lovely dinner, Mary, what a pity you served it cold.'

Grandma exploded. On cue, mother had a funny turn which we all ignored. When the dust settled, dad and I packed our belongings whilst mother sat in the car sulking. We departed, never to be invited again.

*

Four years passed; my mother's constant carping began affecting my dad's health. He began finding the stairs increasingly difficult, then, after a serious heart attack, he was listed for a transplant. To my great relief, they found a suitable donor heart.

Whilst daddy was recovering, mother started going to bingo twice a week, often coming home extremely late. Suspicious, I followed her to the bus stop one evening. A car stopped and mother got in, kissing the driver. Bile rose in my throat and grief seized my heart; I was distraught. I didn't tell dad, nor did I confront my mother lest her inevitable histrionics affected his health. God, I hated her. I

Sweet and Sour

didn't speak to her unless it was strictly necessary. This she put down to teenage grumpiness.

As he recovered, dad started watching football on T.V. something he'd never done before. One evening there was a big game on, dad settled happily in his favourite armchair clutching a beer. He was looking forward eagerly to the game. Coincidentally, mother's 'Bingo' had been cancelled, and her mood was vile. She changed channels with a curt 'why are you forcing me to watch that rubbish?'

Father snatched the remote back, his face puce. 'Piss off and watch the one upstairs you selfish bitch' he bawled. Dad had never even raised his voice to her before let alone swear. Mother was so shocked that she forgot to have a funny turn. After that dad slept in the spare room.

The change in my father's personality became so pronounced that I Googled heart transplants. I discovered that it was not uncommon for a heart recipient to acquire some of the character traits of the donor. Oh, how I blessed that donor.

*

I went to university the following year but came home regularly at weekends. Mother hadn't changed and father looked miserable, often bickering with her. I told him about the affair, but he already knew.

'Since I can't work, Elizabeth, I can't afford to divorce her without selling the house,' he sighed, he looked weary, his eyes sad. 'I'm utterly trapped.'

Two weeks later dad rang to say mother had run off with her to Canada with her lover. My heart sang. The next time I went home there was a new light in dad's eyes. I was overjoyed, but my joy was to be short-lived.

The following spring father's body started to reject his heart. The doctors did all they could, but he died before another organ could be found. I was devastated.

I finished university despite feeling hollow inside; it's what dad would have wanted.

I inherited the house and a large insurance policy, but the place held too many unhappy memories. I decided to sell up and move on. I called in an estate agent. She advised me that the place lacked kerb appeal, so I had the outside painted and the gardens landscaped.

It was the landscapers who found mother's body.

Confrontation

McCord came up to me 'you're on point, O'Sullivan.'

'What? Me again, Sergeant?'

His vulturine eyes gleamed 'yes, O'Sullivan, you again.'

Sergeant Alexander McCord hated my guts. My dog tags said RC (Roman Catholic) He was a Glaswegian Orangeman; hatred of Catholics had been ingested with his mother's milk. He was a veteran of the Korean War and the Malayan emergency he was as big, hard and as ugly as a brick shithouse.

'Why, Sergeant?'

'You were an infantryman in the Territorial Army before you joined up, weren't you?'

'Yes, Sergeant.'

'These lads are artillerymen; they don't have your training.' His sly sneer shouted liar. 'Just keep your fuckin' eyes open, Fenian, I've got a bad feeling about this one.' He turned away before I could make further protest, not that it would have done me any good.

Impin, our Sarawak Ranger interpreter grinned widely at me, his broken yellow teeth making his mouth look like a busted piss pot. 'He fuckin' much love you, Jonny,' he called everyone Jonny. He laughed; it was his idea of a joke.

'Puki' (cunt) I called him, and he laughed again.

The Borneo jungle is stunningly beautiful, but it's a hellish place to hold a war. Leaches, mosquitoes and snakes were only part of the daily nuisances. The unrelenting 33c heat and the 100% humidity were oppressive. Beneath the dark green canopy, it was incredibly noisy. Every damned creature from monkey to maggot seemed to scream at top pitch. At night a different set of creatures started their unrelenting cacophony. It also rained every afternoon to monsoon proportions. The steam rose from the jungle, turning the sky grey then fell as torrential rain, making the rivers swell dangerously.

In 1963, Indonesia adopted a policy of confrontation towards the newly formed Malaysia, sending troops over the border. It was small scale insurgency, not much of a war as wars go. We sneaked about, setting ambushes at border crossings, doing hearts and minds work in the longhouses and kampongs. It was a strategy that paid high dividends.

I went to the front of the patrol as we began to line up. Bombardier Griffin, our second in command, was the next man behind me. He picked up the Bren gun, threw the sling over his shoulder, checked behind him, then nodded at me.

I moved off down the path across the river and away from Pang Ampat our home Kampong.

Sweet and Sour

*

Two hours advance brought us to an area where the bush overgrew the track, obscuring the view ahead. I was about to draw my parang and start hacking when I heard voices just yards away. I signalled contact, and hurriedly shouldered my rifle, guts trembling. They appeared three yards away. It was a Dayak hunting party dressed only in loincloths. I lowered my rifle and smiled. 'Salamat pagi, tuan' (Good morning, friend) I greeted the first man. If they were surprised to see us, they didn't show it. Impin asked if they'd seen any Indonesians; they hadn't. After scrounging some of our tobacco they left, chattering excitedly.

McCord, who had held his peace in front of the Dayaks, stormed up to me, his face like thunder 'You let those guys get right on top of us O'Sullivan, you careless bastard, they could've been Indoes.'

I flared at his injustice. 'Fuck off McCord, try doing point yourself' I spat before I could stop myself.

'Right, O'Sullivan, I'm charging you with gross insubordination. You're for it when we get back.'

I bit my tongue, my hatred festering. My time would come.

The day passed, tense, but uneventful. We laid up off the track behind a clump of giant bamboo just before dark. As my Hexamine stove heated my food, I approached Griffin. 'What's McCord got against me,

Bombardier? I can't believe it's just his sectarian shit.'

Griffin squirmed, taking a long swig of tea before looking me in the eye. 'He reckons you're an orphan, O'Sullivan, 'cos you never get any mail. The other lads all have families, see. There's no bugger to weep for you, is there?'

The old sad-sick feeling of shame burned in me, and my head dropped. I was eleven again, being bullied at school "your dad's a murderer" was the oft-repeated taunt. Dad had killed a man in a drunken brawl. In 1953 a manslaughter conviction was a thing of shame. I saw my mother's gaunt face cowed by years of beatings and intimidation, poor soul. Why she stood by the bugger I'll never know.

I was sixteen when my father came home to resume his violence. He spent most of his wages and mine on drink, always ready with his fists if I protested. On and on it went until one Friday night when I was eighteen, I rebelled. I was chasing girls now, I needed money for that. He stood, hand out, 'wages' he demanded.

'No.'

He raised his fist 'wages, boy, *now*.'

'Fuck off.'

He punched me and the years of pent-up rage and frustration exploded in a red mist. I beat him senseless then gripped his throat, squeezing. Only my mother's screaming pleas stopped me from killing him.

Sweet and Sour

On Monday morning I went to the Army recruiting office and signed on. I had to get out before one of us killed the other. His revenge was to forbid my mother, younger brother and sisters from contacting me.

I returned to the present with a sigh. 'Orphan, eh?' I said, the taste of bile in my mouth, 'shit, when I was growing up, I used to think orphans were lucky buggers.'

Griffin looked me askance; clearly, he didn't believe me. Well, fuck him, and fuck McCord, too. My past was private, my shame not for sharing. I moved away to eat, nursing my resentment.

I stripped off my sodden uniform. 'Olly' Olsen burned the leeches off me with a cigarette. Not bad, only seven of them this time. I did the same for him then I bedded down. McCord took the first watch.

An hour before dawn we stood too. First light was the favourite time for enemy attacks. We watched, listening for changes in the jungle's din that would betray any approach until an hour after dawn.

McCord was nervous, he ordered no stoves and no smoking, so we ate cold rations and drank our chlorinated water. Our mood was foul. No smokes, no brew. God help any bastard who crossed us today. We changed back into our stinking wet uniforms, carefully wrapping our dry stuff in our groundsheets and placing it on top of our kit where it had a chance of staying dry for the night to come. We moved off; I took point.

*

Late morning, the track dropped steeply to a shallow river thirty feet below and 200 yards wide. The Indonesian soldier was sitting on the far bank, leisurely smoking. I signalled contact and McCord joined me. I pointed.

'Seen any more of 'em, O'Sullivan?'

'No sarge' I whispered, 'but he can't be on his own.'

'Right, keep watching, I'll deploy the lads. If he looks like buggering off, slot the bastard.'

I'd never killed before, I didn't want to now, but this was war. I set my sights at 200 yards.

The man got up, filled his water bottle, then, dropping his pants, he shat in the river.

You filthy bastard, I thought, folk downstream have to drink that. I hated him now.

Trousers reinstated, he picked up his gear and moved unhurriedly toward the jungle.

I aimed carefully, gently squeezing the trigger. My rifle kicked into my shoulder the shot sounding as loud as a cannon.

The man fell to his knees then sagged over on his side.

In the eery silence that followed, I felt nothing.

We waited. The jungle reassumed its usual clamour.

Sweet and Sour

Nothing happened.

After an hour, McCord said 'I reckon they've fucked off.'

I knew what was coming next.

'Right, O'Sullivan, go across and scout around. We'll cover you.'

Reluctantly, I slid down the bank. As I stepped from the jungle's dark protective greenness into the calf-deep water the sun illuminated me like a target in a shooting gallery. My knees trembled, and my guts clenched as I imagined bullets ripping through me, shredding my insides. I gripped my rifle tightly to stop my hands from shaking. I started across, feeling naked, expecting every step to be my last.

The bullets didn't come.

On the opposite bank, there was a large rock at the water's edge. I crouched behind it and tossed a grenade up the track. It detonated. There was no reaction, so I advanced, passing the dead soldier, his sightless eyes staring at me. 'You shouldn't have shit in the river, cunt' I told him trying to assuage my guilty pang.

In the trees, there were five dead fires and one still faintly smouldering. Judging by the flattened brush, I reckoned there'd been twenty-five or thirty of them. It looked like McCord was right. I signalled all clear.

Griffin was almost across when his head exploded in a gout of gore, and he flopped like a puppet with cut strings, his face expressionless. The firing came from a small scrub-covered spur that jutted into the river seventy-five yards upstream.

The lads ran for cover, firing as they went. McCord snatched up Griffin's Bren gun sending a stream of bullets into the enemy position, suppressing their fire. 'Move lads, move!' he bawled. I could see bullets splashing around him, but he just stood there calmly firing, keeping their heads down until the last bloke was across. Turning bank-wards he was hit in the thigh and sat down abruptly, screaming obscenities whilst changing his magazine. He sat there firing and cursing, unable to move, his blood staining the shallow water.

Christ alone knows why I ran out. The voice in my head screamed idiot, idiot, fuckin' idiot! But my legs kept pumping. It was only fifteen yards or so, but it felt like fifteen miles.

McCord was heavier than I had expected what with the weight of his pack and the Bren I struggled to lift him. I managed to drag his left arm over my shoulder and get him upright. He continued squirting short, accurate bursts, forcing the enemy to duck. 'Come on yer bastard' I yelled my voice panicked.

We staggered into cover, my heart bursting, my breath rasping. Relief and anger flooded me in equal measure. I dropped him, reaching for my field dressing.

Sweet and Sour

'They're sending in the Ghurkhas by chopper, lads' Olsen yelled. He'd been on the radio and the bloody thing had worked for once.

The enemy now knew how few we were and left the spur. We could hear them advancing through the brush. Could we hold out until reinforcements arrived?

We couldn't go back, and we couldn't go on, leaving the enemy behind us and enemy territory in front.

An ashen-faced McCord, his wound dressed, manned the Bren gun, waiting. They fired wildly, spasmodically through the brush, seeming reluctant to press home an attack. If they did, we were dead.

McCord looked at me 'in case we don't make it, O'Sullivan, thanks.' he muttered.

'Yeah, right,' I told him sourly. 'Good job you're not a fuckin' orphan, McCord.' His mouth fell agape.

After fifteen minutes blind sniping, the enemy's rate of fire suddenly increased; they were advancing. Where the hell were those Ghurkhas?

We fired at any movement we saw as a volley ripped out of the jungle. Wood splinters and earth flew but miraculously none of us was hit. I was the only bloke with grenades, the others had never trained on them. I threw my last one as far into the bush as I could and was rewarded with screams.

And then their firing stopped as the distant slapping of helicopter blades was heard. One minute later three Wessex Helicopters flew low over the trees to hover a few feet above the river disgorging running Ghurkhas.

The enemy vanished into the jungle. It was over.

We loaded Griffin's body aboard the nearest chopper and McCord was hoisted in after him to lie on the floor wincing. The last thing he said to me was 'take charge, O'Sullivan, get the lads aboard the other choppers.' Then his helicopter lifted off blasting the pungent stink of burnt kerosene and blowing my jungle hat into the river. McCord's hand waved through the open door. I waved back wearily, the adrenaline no longer surging, my hatred for him expunged.

Out of Habit

Monica is sitting at the bar her long jeans-clad legs crossed, her foot swinging gently to the music. She is drinking alone, a wistful smile on her pink lips.

He enters, does a double-take then sidles up near, but not too close to her. Ordering a rum and coke, he eyes her obliquely, assessing her with care. He takes a long swig of his drink while he plucks up his courage. His expression changes as he decides to take a chance and, turning towards her, he smiles broadly. 'So, this is where you hang out when you're not modelling, eh?'

She laughs at his cheesy chat-up line 'Modelling? I wish!'

She accepts a drink with a good-natured grin, her body language open. Monica is an attentive listener, tilting her head slightly, her smiling eyes holding his as he talks. He tells her his name is Rodrigo, he's divorced, no kids, he hails from Milan. He's in town for a few days on business; it's clear he's lonely. He's forty-two, same as her. She eyes his lithe body and decides he'll suit her purpose nicely.

Rodrigo notices the white patch on her finger where a ring had recently been. 'What about you, Monica? Are you married, got a bloke?'

Her mouth turns down at the corners, 'kinda married, sort of, you might say…' she breaks off, reluctant to talk about it.

'Kinda? Like stuck with an older man or something?'

She grimaced 'yes, an incredibly old man I'm afraid.'

Rodrigo is curious and starts asking questions about her relationship. She holds up her hand 'Look, Rodrigo, I don't make a habit of this, I can only get away very infrequently.' She strokes his hand, smiling knowingly. 'We both know what we need so let's just enjoy the evening, OK?'

He's reluctant to let it go, he knows she's hiding something and he's curious, but Rodrigo hasn't had sex for three months; he keeps his peace.

They dance. Another drink then they dance again. She's as sensuous as a serpent writhing around him. His needs become urgent, overriding his curiosity. One more drink and then they leave.

*

In his hotel room, Monica is eager as he slips off her blouse and jeans. She responds, fiercely tugging his belt free, whimpering with anticipation as she slides his zip down.

Sweet and Sour

They have wild sex three times before dawn, leaving the bed looking like a battlefield.

She lay awake for a long time afterwards, sexually replete but with her conscience plaguing her. This was the fifth time she'd done it in recent years. Cheating did not come naturally to her, but her needs slowly increased until she was desperate. Masturbation helped but it was not enough. Dammit, she thought, wiping her eyes on the sheet, every red-blooded woman needs sex, has a *right* to sex. Pushing away her guilt, with and with a final sniff, she fell into a fitful sleep her head on his chest.

*

As the sky begins to lighten, Monica rises, dressing hurriedly, gasping as she drops a shoe.

'Where are you going, Monica?'

Her heart sinks, she had hoped to slip away and leave him sleeping. She cringes inwardly, this was going to be awkward 'I have to get back before I'm missed, Rodrigo.'

He rises and stands between her and the door 'last night was incredible, Monica, I must see you again, please.'

'I can't Rodrigo, I told you that last night, please, let me go.'

He grabs her wrist, his face pained. 'Please' he pleads 'give me your number, an address, anything.'

'No, Rodrigo, I can't. Please, let me go.'

His eyes set hard 'No, I can't, I won't, not until you promise to see me again.'

A distant clock starts striking the three-quarter hour, her mouth trembles and a tear starts down her cheek, she's desperate now. 'OK, Rodrigo, OK, please let me go and I'll see you at ten a.m. at the pavement café across from St Marks, I swear.'

'You swear?'

She touches the small gold crucifix hanging around her neck 'yes.'

Reluctantly he accepts this and she leaves.

10 a.m. Monica covertly observed him from across the street. He's sitting at a pavement table, an untouched coffee before him, glancing at his watch.

As the last chime of St Marks clock fades, he rises, looking anxiously into the face of each passing woman.

It's a terrible risk, but she has sworn to see him and must keep her promise. Monica takes a deep breath, butterflies dancing in her stomach and crosses the road ten metres up the pavement from him. She walks up, glancing into his face, smiling shyly. He responds with a curt nod, sidestepping her as he gazes up the street into the distance. She passes him, breathing a deep sigh of relief. She has kept her promise. Turning the corner, she lowers her face against a chill wind, pulling her wimple more closely around her head as she hurries back to the convent.

Rat Pie

Why would anyone eat a rat? I mean, seriously, why would any sane, rational person kill, cook and eat a rat?

As a ten-year-old, I was attending the funeral of an elderly great aunt when I noticed a strange old man in a Harris tweed jacket and baggy flannels staring at me. He was tall, his frame sturdy, his face careworn and tanned to the colour of my brown Sunday shoes. It was his rheumy blue eyes that struck me most, they looked so kindly and yet so sad. It was as though he'd witnessed every sadness this world had to offer.

'Who's that?' I asked my father, nudging and pointing rudely.

My Father looked in his direction his face bleak 'Oh, him, he's a relative…. of sorts.'

'What sort of relative is he, daddy?' I asked, my curiosity aroused. I wondered why I had not seen or even heard of him before now and what the term a relative of sorts meant. Either he was a relative or he wasn't.

'Be quiet, you're in church, show some respect' I was admonished.

Later, outside the church, I saw my father talking to the old man. Dad was fidgeting, shifting his weight from one foot to the other His hands were making vague gestures, his voice a mumble. My mother was engaged talking to the vicar in a group with her sisters my aunts Florence and Doris. She kept stealing furtive glances in my father's direction. I sneaked closer to hear what dad was saying. I was puzzled to hear dad mumble 'sorry dad, you know how they are, best if you didn't come back.'

The old man nodded looking even sadder than before 'Aye, son, no matter, I'll be away then.' He turned and strode away down the church path. He didn't look like a man rejected, his walk was march-like, his head high and his shoulders square. Under the lychgate, he stopped and looked back briefly. At the distance, I couldn't be sure, but I thought there was a tear in his eye. Then he turned and quickly walked away.

'Who is he, daddy?' I asked, why did you call him dad? Why did he call you son?'

My father's face reddened 'how long have you been listening, Tony?'

I cringed inwardly as though I'd been caught in some crime, my lips trembled. 'Just now daddy' I said hurriedly 'I came to see how much longer we'd be here.' It was a white lie, of course, but it was better than saying I was curious and wanted to listen in.

My father's face sagged, and his shoulders slumped. 'I suppose I should have told you before now.' He squirmed and looked towards my mother

Sweet and Sour

who was still in conversation with the vicar. 'Oh, hell,' he said, the air left his lips in a long sigh, 'the old man is my father, your granddad but he's not a nice person to know, no one likes him.'

'He looked all right to me' I said, 'he looked sad, too.'

'What have you told him, Paul?' my mother had come up suddenly behind us, her lips were tightly pursed, eyebrows arched, her eyes were as small and hard as two dried peas. It was a look I knew well. Mother was seriously displeased. My knees started to shake, there was always a heavy price to pay for incurring her displeasure.

When we got home from the wake, I was sent for, and the outcast of the family was explained to me.

'He's a sewer man for the council and smells abdominally most of the time' my mother said, 'and his eating habits are utterly disgusting.' the corners of her mouth turned down in sharp points. 'He eats vermin.'

'What's vermin, mum?'

'It's rats and pigeons and....'my father joined in.

'That's enough' mum snapped 'he doesn't need to hear the details.'

Dad looked crestfallen.

'We only tolerated him at the funeral because your great aunt Elsie was his sister' mother rasped 'so just forget about him and never, and I mean *never* mention him at school, or to anyone, understand?'

I didn't understand, but I nodded anyway. When my parents were this serious, I knew better than to argue.

And so, the incident passed into history, I was an active boy, I did sports after school and joined a boys club my dad had been a member of. There, I learned boxing and how to keep fit. I never forgot the about my sad granddad although I never dared mention him again.

Time passed and shortly after my thirteenth birthday I saw my Granddad again. He was replacing a sewer lid outside our school. I knew I'd get in trouble if I was caught, but I followed him to his home, a rundown terrace in an area my mother said was full of undesirables, whatever undesirables were. I waited until he had gone inside then I screwed up my courage, walked up to his door and knocked.

He looked down at me, frowning. I could tell he knew who I was.

'What do you want, lad?' His voice was gruff. He forced a cough to clear his throat 'do your parents know you're here?'

'No, they don't.'

'You'll be in trouble if they find out' he said his face hard, his eyes blank.

'I don't care I said, puffing out my chest 'you're my granddad, aren't you?' He nodded. I was desperate to know everything about him. 'Why are you dirty, why do you eat rats?' I blurted.

Sweet and Sour

I thought I saw the hint of a smile 'you'd best come in for a minute' he said and stepped aside to allow me into the small hall. The house was surprisingly neat, not a trace of dirt anywhere and the only smell that of lavender. What was I expecting of this man who ate rats? Filth everywhere? A terrible stench? I suppose I did.

'A cup of tea' he asked, or elderflower cordial?'

I made a fool of myself. 'what's it made of? I asked nervously before I even stopped to think.

He laughed, exposing healthy white teeth while his kindly blue eyes danced in his wrinkled face, 'Well, I usually make tea with a teabag and the cordial with elderflowers. The clue's in the name.' he said with a big grin.

Seated on an old but clean and comfortable sofa sipping his very tasty cordial I was full of questions, but I didn't know where or how to start, or even if I should start, after all, I hadn't been invited. He sensed my dilemma.

'What did they tell you about me, Tony?' he asked.

Being a tactless little brat, I ploughed straight in 'I've been told that you're not a nice person, that nobody likes you because you smell and eat vermin.'

'Yes, child, most of that is true' he said nodding slowly My work clothes smell because I work down sewers, but I keep them outside in the outhouse where I breed my rats.'

'Why do you eat rats?' I asked, 'there's plenty of meat in the shops.'

'I have my reasons, reasons which are none of anyone's business but mine.'

I had been rebuffed, but not in a nasty way. His tone was even, his voice gentle. The sad look was back in his eye. 'I brought your dad up on food like that and look what a big, fine and strong man he grew into.'

I pressed him on the matter, but he closed down on me saying he'd said too much already.

I went to see him once a week after that without telling my parents but, inevitably, they found out. Mother went ape. They tried to forbid me to go but I showed defiance 'I'll tell everyone that he's my granddad if you don't let me go' I told them angrily. 'He's a nice old man and I like him.'

Mother's face was as sour as a lemon for ages after that, but they didn't try to stop me for fear I'd carry out my threat and tell people. I had, however, strict instructions never to eat any food he may offer me.

Growing up, I'd always been a rebellious little shit, so, to celebrate my fourteenth birthday, I tasted my first rat and bacon pie. It was delicious. I got to know my grandfather better with every visit, each time learning a bit more about this shy, gentle old man. However, he was very reluctant to talk about his

Sweet and Sour

past so getting information was extremely difficult, but, little by little, I drew him out.

As a young man, Granddad had been engaged to my grandmother at the start of World War two. He was among the first to volunteer. The leaving celebrations got a bit heavy and as a result, my grandma got pregnant with my father. Like so many wartime stories, theirs was to end in tragedy. Shortly after she gave birth to my dad, grandma was run over and killed by a car the blackout, she was just twenty-one. The only picture in granddad's house was an old, faded photo of my grandmother. She had been beautiful. He had never looked at another woman again.

On his eightieth birthday, I took a bottle of granddad's favourite whiskey to celebrate. I must admit I used every trick I knew to get him a little drunk and he let his defences drop at last.

What I found was heart-breaking. Granddad was captured in Singapore by the Japanese and sent to work on the Burma railway. There, he saw many of his comrades die of dysentery, malnutrition, beaten or bayonetted to death by the guards. 'If we got too weak to work' he said 'they just got rid of us' I could tell he didn't want to remember as tears formed in his eyes when he spoke of those times. I thought it was important that I should know, and that everyone should know about the terrible suffering of those unfortunate men.

'Did they feed you on rats, granddad?' I asked incredulously.

'No lad, just a small bowl of thin rice gruel a day. We started eating rats, snakes and any damned thing we could get our hands on' he told me. 'At first, the Japs stopped us doing it until they realised that the ones of us that ate 'jungle meat' as we called it, were stronger and could work harder, so they turned a blind eye.'

Granddad went on to explain that when he came home from the war, it took a long while for him to become rehabilitated. He was eventually demobilised into a country in dire straits. Food was strictly rationed, and jobs were scarce for unskilled men like him. He took any work he could find, no matter how poorly paid. Eventually, he got a job with the local council as a sewer man. The pay was abysmal, and he had my father to bring up on his own.

'All the kids in the street were puny and undernourished' he told me 'I didn't want that for your dad. My workplace was teeming with rats and so I thought why not? I had survived when so many perished due to eating whatever we could catch.' He smiled and his old eyes twinkled he said 'I was awful at cooking until I found a recipe book on cooking game in a second-hand bookshop. I thought rats were no different to game, just smaller, so I spent a whole tuppence on that book. I never told your dad what the meat it was, I just called it wild meat pie or country

Sweet and Sour

stew. He didn't ask and I didn't tell. He laughed, genuinely amused, 'you see, Tony, these things are purely a matter of perception. In this country, we eat fish, lamb, beef, pork, game and poultry. You mention eating horse meat and everyone freaks out. Why? A horse is just a quadruped same as a cow. The French eat horsemeat, and nobody bats an eye.'

He went on to tell me that his neighbours grew suspicious when delicious cooking smells wafted from his kitchen and he was accused of buying black-market meat, a criminal offence in those days.

'How can a shit shoveller like you afford fresh meat every day?' they asked me Granddad said. 'Someone sneaked around and discovered my secret and after that, I was shunned. 'I thought bugger 'em, they don't know what it is to starve, to be truly hungry. After a while, it didn't bother me or your dad. I developed a taste for rats and started breeding my own. They were bigger, cleaner and had more flavour. When my Paul, got bullied at school, I made him join a boys' club and learn to box. The bullying soon stopped after he knocked some heads together.'

On my next visit, I got Granddad talking about my dad. 'He was a grand lad' he said 'until he went to do his Army National Service. He saw another, better side to life, then. He worked in the officers' mess as a waiter. Then he met your mother who was what they call these days upwardly mobile.' He sighed, 'she disliked me from the off. A sewer man was not a person she wanted in her close family. She married your dad anyway. Up North, in secret it was. Well, secret from me anyhow.' There was no bitterness in him, just an acceptance of that's how things were.

I grew to love that old man dearly, he taught me so much about life. His philosophy was a simple one. Don't rale against things you can't change. Learn to accept without judgement that people are the way they are because of their life's circumstances. He even learned to forgive his Japanese captors eventually. He told me hatred was like picking hot coals out of a fire with your bare hands to throw at those you hated. He also taught me to always question things. 'Ask why something has to be so and why can't it be different.' he told me. 'Always listen to others but draw your own conclusions.' It was advice that has stood me well.

It was granddad who sparked my interest in cooking. His hedgehog Wellington stuffed with wild sweet chestnuts was scrumptious He did a roadkill rabbit roulade that you could have served in a top-class restaurant.

And so, as I grew older, I went to catering college where I met my wife, Jean. We worked in hotel kitchens for years while saving for our dream of striking out on our own.

We opened our restaurant on my thirtieth birthday. We called it The Fat Rat, which everyone thought was hilarious. We specialised in game and poultry, it was

Sweet and Sour

an instant success, developing a great reputation and eventually a Michelin star.

In the last year of his life, granddad took to watching arty-farty cooking programmes on TV. He noticed that modern chefs left their meat quite pink, and he started doing the same. I warned him not to eat rare rat, but he wouldn't listen. He caught dysentery and died after a short illness, mind you, he was ninety-two.

The family moaned about funeral expenses until I assured them Jean and I would cover the costs. They cheered up even more when I told them I'd be serving champagne and a lavish meal at my home after the funeral.

Ceremony over, the mourners gathered at my house where we toasted granddad in fine vintage champagne. I'd never seen so many of my relatives gathered in one place before all quaffing my drink and stuffing themselves with canapes.

We sat down to a splendid meal, the wine flowed, and granddad would have been embarrassed to hear so many relatives all speaking well of him for a change. Afterwards, I tapped my wineglass with a fork to command silence.

I thanked them for coming. 'You know,' I said 'It was granddad who encouraged me to go into catering, hence my present prosperity. He it was who taught me that everything is just a matter of perception.' Heads nodded sagely as they sipped my aged cognac. 'Take this meal instance' I said. 'The starter, Pate Au Sauvage, I made that with the hearts, livers and gizzards of feral pigeon. The Game pie was a mixture of rat, roadkill rabbit and hedgehog in a hawthorn sauce.'

I never got as far as describing the sweet. Each of my relatives paled, looking like they'd just pulled a squelchy turd from a lucky dip.

It cost me a hundred and fifty pounds to have our carpets steam cleaned and they still carry a slight pong of puke but, by God, it was worth it.

Matter of Luck

'Hell, killed by his hobby, how unlucky was that, Benny?'
'For God's sake, Daffid, don't bloody start with that luck crap, and keep your end of the stretcher up, will you? Benny sighed as a wave of depression washed through him. How many more times would he be detailed to carry some poor sod's body back for burial? How could a man be so stupid as to risk his life to see a bird no matter how rare it was? And him a captain, too.

They stumbled along the communication trench lit only by dim oil lamps ten yards apart. This way they could avoid the deadly German sniper who had plagued them for over a week now. The man was uncannily accurate, being able to put a bullet through a cigarette glow if someone was careless enough to expose one.

The stretcher's passenger was one Captain Horatio Algenon Beardsley aged twenty-three, the late son of a Kent clergyman. He had met his end indulging his passion for bird watching. A keen twitcher, he had mumbled something about an extremely rare warbler, his eyes alight with enthusiasm. He had risked a glance over the parapet through his binoculars despite

Benny's shouted warning. Five seconds later the sniper got him.

They reached the aid post and addressed the orderly Sergeant 'Officer, Sarge. Dead.'

'Put him behind the post lads, the left-hand tent is for officers. Take a ten-minute smoke break then get yourselves back, OK?'

They smoked in silence, each with his own thoughts of their late passenger. He had been a decent sort, the captain, reading and writing letters for the illiterate among them. He was always trying to make trench life a little better for his men. Then, in a moment of sheer madness, he'd lost his life.

They made their way back wearily, Benny had to be up before first light to take up his sniper position unseen. They bade each other good night and turned in.

*

Daffid Jones fingered the lucky rabbit's foot that hung around his neck. He lit a cigarette and, leaning against the trench wall, exhaling smoke into the warm September breeze. 'If he'd had one of these, the captain would still be with us, Benny.'

Benny Thomas looked at the long lugubrious face of Daffid, his companion of the last four years 'I've told you before, Daffid, I don't believe in that nonsense, I've survived the same four years as you without one.'

Sweet and Sour

'Ah yes, but you've been wounded, I haven't. Anyway, when are you going to get that bloody sniper? He's had three of us this week already.'

Benny's mouth turned down at the corners, and he looked away, embarrassed. 'Well, I've had one of theirs, a bloody Major, too.' he said defensively.

It was September 1918, the war could not last much longer, everyone knew the Hun was on the run. And today even the artillery had slowed to desultory firing. It was as though the gunners on either side were enjoying the Indian summer and couldn't be bothered humping all those heavy shells. The only real problem they had now was the sniper.

'I've got him down to two areas he uses' Benny said 'it's just a matter of pinpointing the bugger. With a bit of luck, I'll have him tomorrow.' As soon as the words left his mouth, Benny could have bitten his tongue off. Why the hell had he mentioned luck?

'I've told you, Benny, you should get one of these.' He held up the furry little paw with its shiny silver mounting that he polished daily with a near-religious fervour. 'There's nothing better for luck, I can't understand why everyone doesn't have one.'

Benny guffawed his good humour restored. 'Did it ever occur to you, Daffid, that the rabbit had four of 'em? Didn't do him much good, did they?'

Daffid shook his head looking sour 'You have to believe, see? No good if you don't believe, boyo.' Then he smiled at Benny, his craggy face and broken teeth making him look like a benevolent gargoyle. 'Look, you just rub this rabbit's foot now and watch your luck change. You'll get that sniper for sure.'

Benny grinned broadly his bright blue eyes sparkling in his weathered face. He loved his superstitious friend who'd shared four years of hell with him. They had often argued fiercely over inconsequential things as soldiers do, but it had been Daffid who had run into no man's land and dragged him back when he was wounded.

'OK, then, you crazy Welshman if it'll shut you up.' Benny rubbed the tiny appendage, 'happy now?'

Daffid smiled 'Just you wait and see, Benny.'

'Yeah, right.' Benny got up, 'must go and clean my rifle, Daffid. See you later.'

*

The next day, Benny lay in a shallow shell scrape under a camouflaged tarpaulin. It was hot and uncomfortable. Flies and insects buzzed and bit, and his bladder was uncomfortably full, but he couldn't afford to move more than a few inches lest he give away his position. He was some twenty yards behind the trench. Too many snipers had died in no man's land where the enemy gave most scrutiny. He looked at the hillock two hundred yards away and slightly to his right. I know you're up there, Fritz he thought, just make one wrong move, that's all.

The sun rose high above the shell shattered landscape and Daffid sat on an ammunition ledge

Sweet and Sour

reading his newly arrived letter. It was bad news. His beloved grandmother, who had given him his lucky rabbit's foot, had passed away.

With a tear in his eye, Daffid withdrew the charm from his shirt and kiss it, holding it up to the heavens. The silver top glinted brightly in the noonday sun.

On his hillock, Corporal Uwe Gintz saw the gleam through the gap in the warped trench boards. It took him only a few seconds to aim and fire. The gleam disappeared instantly. Hans smiled his satisfaction; another dumb Tommy had made his last mistake.

Uwe drew his lucky rabbit's foot from under his tunic, stroked it and held it up, smiling.

Two hundred yards away Benny saw the flash of sun on silver. He aimed carefully and squeezed the trigger, feeling the rifle kick into his shoulder. 'Gotcha, Fritz' he muttered. A mixture of relief and satisfaction surged through him, tempered by a sigh. 'Now I suppose I'll have to listen to Daffid banging on about lucky bloody rabbits' feet all day,'

The Devil's Doorbell

'Masturbation' roared Father Murphy the preying priest 'is the eighth deadly sin. Sexual satisfaction through self-stimulation is abhorrent in the sight of the Lord.'

The girls in our class blushed to their roots, we boys looked down at our shuffling feet willing the ground to open and swallow us. Our guilty faces gave us away for the wanton wankers we were.

'Yes, all of you, for I know you girls do it, too,' he stared at Molly Molloy sitting next to me. She stared boldly back. 'When you girls play with that little button between your legs, you're ringing the devil's doorbell and he will surely let you in.'

Murphy glowered, I thought, directly at me and Molly. I had just pulled myself off in the boys' toilets before this very lesson. Well, Molly Molloy had such beautiful blouse bustin' boobs and her arse moved like a melody. She was so damn cute, I mean, what's a fourteen-year-old lad to do?

'You boys with your lustful, lecherous longings, pulling your penises over pictures of Marilyn Monroe and other such strumpets, you'll burn in hell for your wicked desires.' He paused for effect before

Sweet and Sour

continuing his rant. 'Know this: God can see you. He knows the contents of your soul.'

Molly nudged my elbow 'Look at his trousers' she whispered, 'he's got a hard-on.'

I looked. There was a bit of a bulge at the front, but I couldn't tell for certain. Anyway, what would Molly know about hard-on's she was younger than me. 'How can you be sure?' I asked doubtfully.

'Cos my big brother's trousers look like that before he takes his girlfriend up to his room to play records' she said, 'I can hear them from my room.'

'The records?'

'No, what they are getting up to, silly.'

'Oh,' I said, embarrassed by this revelation. I was lost for words.

Then Molly leaned into my ear and whispered 'That's when I ring the Devil's doorbell' she giggled, enjoying my discomfiture. 'What makes you do it?' she asked cheekily.

'I don't do it' I fibbed, 'it's impure and I'd have to tell Father at confession.'

'Liar' she chided 'you lent my cousin George a picture of a naked lady, I saw it in his room.'

'You two!' Murphy bawled pointing a bony forefinger at us, 'out here.'

We went before the priest, I was trembling with fear, my stomach churning.

He gazed at us for a moment his rheumy eyes seemed to bore into the very core of my being 'What were you talking about that's more important than saving your immortal souls?'

'Masturbation, Father' said Molly brazenly, 'and how best to do it.'

I thought the spluttering Murphy would die of apoplexy on the spot. His face turned scarlet, and his thin lips were flecked with spittle. He shook from head to toe. 'Get out' he screamed pointing at the classroom door 'you two are beyond redemption. Get out the pair of you.'

Molly turned at the door 'I hope you enjoy that hard-on Father' she shouted, 'my mum says you're the biggest wanker this parish has ever had,' with that we turned and fled.

We took the long cut home through the woods dawdling and chatting in the warm summer sunshine. Molly was so sweet, her smile divine. She wheedled my secrets out of me, making me confess to galloping my maggot.

We stopped near a grassy bank under a huge oak 'let's sit for a bit' she said. 'it's too soon to go home.' I sat next to her as close as I dared, stealing surreptitious glances at her tits, hoping she wouldn't notice, but she did of course.

'Do you like 'em?' She stuck her chest out grinning mischievously.

I dropped my gaze, reddening 'er…yeah, 'course I do. I like all of you, Molly.'

Sweet and Sour

She lifted my face and kissed me, oh the joy that surged through me. My pulse raced and I thought my heart would burst through my chest. I felt myself getting hard.

When she gently broke away, she was breathing heavily. She looked down at my trousers 'You're feeling randy, aren't you?'

'Er... yes,' I said.

'Me, too. Look,' she said, 'why don't you do it for me and I'll do it to you?'

I couldn't believe my ears 'are you serious?' I asked as a wonderful shock jolted my penis.

She smiled and took her knickers off before stroking my growing bulge. I was lost. She guided my trembling, virgin hand to the Devil's doorbell and I rang it for her good. She fumbled inexpertly with my young hardness, and I showed her how to please it.

It didn't take long for either of us.

That was my first sexual experience with a girl. I could have had many more with Molly in later life as she went on to great things. In 1965, at the ripe old age of twenty-three, she opened the first massage parlour in the county, bless her. She named it "The Devil's Door." The doorbell surround was shaped like female genitalia, you can guess what part of that was the bell push.

Postscript:

Father Murphy was later 'moved on' by the church after what was described as an 'unfortunate incident' with a girl in the class below ours.

Sweet and Sour

Banjaxed

The most exciting day of my life was the day I was murdered.

The sun was bright, blessing the morning with spring warmth that foretold summer. The trees were newly leafing, and the scent of blossom filled the park.

'Do you want another game, John?' I asked.

John smiled a little ruefully 'two defeats are enough for one morning, Alan' he said, packing his bowls away. 'Besides, I'm going to my son's house for lunch, a rare treat these days.'

It was such a lovely morning that I was reluctant to return to my bachelor pad. 'OK, I'll just practice on my own for a half-hour.'

I took a deep, satisfying breath of the scented air and looked around. The only other people present were three youths huddled on a bench in an alcove, their hoods up, their faces down.

They had a conspiratorial air about them resembling mediaeval inquisition monks in conference except for the billowing pall of cannabis smoke.

I turned my back on them and sent my jack out, watching carefully to see how it ran. I followed it with my first bowl and was pleased as it slowed and stopped only six inches from its target. I stooped to pick up my second bowl. It wasn't there.

'Hey, granddad, I want der watch, innit.'

I turned to see a youth maybe fifteen or sixteen standing a couple of feet away scowling from beneath his hoodie, holding my bowl. He was a skinny runty looking little bugger. I smiled at him, remembering my own wayward youth. 'You've got good taste lad,' I told him, holding up my left arm to better display my pride and joy. 'This is thirty grand's worth of unfencible goods' I said, 'it'll get you caught so fast you'll be dizzy.'

He jumped at me then and I saw to my horror he was swinging the bowl at my head. Too late I raised a defensive arm, my sixty-nine-year-old reflexes being far too slow.

Two pounds eight ounces of lignum vitae crashed into my cranium; I felt a dull thud then searing pain filled my entire body as I sank to the greensward. My vision faded away as a wave of weariness engulfed me, but I could still hear. An excited voice cried 'Yer've topped 'im, Jason, grab the watch, let's fuck off quick.'

*

'Hiya Alan, welcome to the hereafter.'

I sat up; the pain was gone. Before me, sitting cross-legged two feet above the turf was a creature that was a cross between a pixie and a leprechaun but dressed conventionally in jeans and a jumper. 'Who

Sweet and Sour

the devil are you?' I asked, unable to understand what I saw.

'I'm Banjax, your guardian demon.' He smiled, 'I've been looking after you all your life.'

I looked around me, bemused, the park was still there only more so. Every plant was more vibrant, more colourful than I had ever seen them before. The grass glowed iridescently, and the birdsong held a more joyful note than I'd ever before heard.

He was speaking again. 'By the way, we don't use the word devil here, it encourages a negative image and upsets the snowflakes.' He grinned at my puzzlement, 'please, Alan, do move away from your corpse, it looks awful, and you don't need it anymore.'

I glanced down at myself and grimaced. I did indeed look ugly with my gaunt yellow/white face and blood oozing from my nose and ears. I moved a few yards away and turned my back on it. So, I was dead, and this creature was my contact in a hereafter that I'd never believed in. If he was a devil come to escort me to the eternal flames, he was a lot friendlier than I had expected.

'I've heard of guardian angels, Banjax,' I said, 'but guardian demons? That's a new one on me, have you come to take me to hell, then?'

His laughter tinkled like a silver windchime 'Hell? There's no such place mate nor is there the religious folk's idea of heaven either.'

'What then?' I was truly puzzled.

'It works like this, Alan: There are several categories of people and certain types of guardians looking after them. The good folk have guardian angels. The bad ones get demons. You, nefarious bugger that you are, have got me.' He grinned, his broken boot face radiating mischief. 'After a year with me, we'll see where you'd fit in best.'

'So, I'm an apprentice demon, then?'

'Yes. We demon's fall into three classes: Lucifer class, they look after the wars and famine, you know, the heavy stuff. Then there is the Beelzebub class, they look after the really nasty people, the murderers, rapists, bankers, politicians, etc.'

'Which class are you, then?' I asked.

'I'm Mammon class, we look after the greedy buggers like you, the conmen, grifters, gamblers, prostitutes et al.'

'I was a good con artist' I told him proudly. 'I never robbed the weak or destitute unlike some. I stuck to the greedy sods with more brass than brains.'

The grin on his ugly face was huge, making his head look like it was about to split in half. 'Oh, give it a rest, Alan,' he chortled 'you'll be telling me you were Robin bleeding Hood next.'

I grimaced 'No, I had class, that's all. I mean, why rob a poor mug when you can rob a rich one? I did well, and never did a day in jail.'

Sweet and Sour

'That's because you always listened to me, Alan. Every time I whispered in your ear you did as I suggested. I was so proud of you.'

'It was you?'

'Yup, I gave you the idea of selling that swamp in Argentina as prime building land to those idiots who thought they were ripping you off.'

'Wow, I made a million and a half from that, even though I had to live in Spain for a while.'

'The thing is, now you're dead, you can join me and have fun spreading fuckery for a whole year before we have to move on.'

'Really?'

'Yes, take that little shit who just killed you, we could introduce him to an undercover copper he believes is a fence.'

'Won't his demon warn him?'

'Yes, of course, but he won't listen, his sort never does. And your ex-wife who buggered off with your best mate and a pile of your money, we could dream up some cool stuff for them.'

So, I became an apprentice demon. For the next year, we visited buggeration upon my enemies. Bad investments, STD's and income tax inspectors were standard reprisals. My ex got special treatment. A dead cat under her floorboards.

The stink left her on the brink of despair. Every time she thought she'd located the smell we moved the corpse. Exasperated, they moved to a new house at huge expense, then we sent them a plague of rats, it was fun hearing her hysterical screams.

Banjax got a female demon to phone, asking for her partner in a slinky voice. That drove her into a fury that she usually reserved for me. She went at her new man until the poor bugger could take no more. He packed his bags one night and cleared off, forcing her to sell the house and work for a living for the first time in her life. Boy, was I having fun!

Banjax and I spread fuckery far and wide, mischief and mayhem were our watchwords.

I was planning some skulduggery to visit on my parish priest, a sanctimonious hypocrite with a weakness for choirboys when the day went dark. I heard Banjax crying.

*

It started to get light again and I could hear voices. Then I saw a pale blob which slowly turned into a white-coated man peering down at me. He turned to someone behind him 'I think he's wakening' he said. 'Miracles do happen.'

I was bemused. I tried to talk but my mouth was dry, my throat sore. I worked my mouth for a while, swallowing painfully. 'Where's Banjax?' I finally managed.

The man ignored me and continued speaking to the person behind him 'He'll be very confused for a while, just ignore what he says, these cases take time.'

Sweet and Sour

My head felt like an anvil with an enthusiastic blacksmith working on it. My blood started to boil. 'Confused my arse,' I croaked 'where's my guardian demon?'

The man bent and shone a torch into each of my eyes in turn then started talking medico-babble to the person behind him.

For three days I came and went and then one bright morning they took several wires from me and sat me up. I was alive.

Bernie O'Carroll, a lovely Irish nurse, oversaw my recovery. She explained that I'd had a fractured skull and a severe bleed on the brain, that I'd been in a coma for a year. 'You died three times on the operating table she said, 'but somehow they brought you back again.'

I closed my eyes as despair washed through me. I didn't want to be brought back again; I was having too much fun with Banjax.

'So, I'll live then?'

'Yes. They had to work like demons on you, Alan, and I thought you were banjaxed, but you pulled through.'

When she said this, I knew my guardian demon was still with me, putting words into her mouth.

'Banjaxed indeed' I said feeling happy once again.

The Cougar's Claws

Her eyes widened and a wicked smile played briefly on her full lips. Well now, she thought, who would have believed it? Old stick-in-the-mud and his missus deviating from their routine. She watched as Peter's parents boarded the King's Lynne train. It was only Thursday; they usually went on Friday. Yes, oh yes, this was indeed a golden opportunity, the boy would be alone. She felt herself beginning to dampen her underwear in anticipation of the pleasure to come.

Returning quickly to her car, Amelia retrieved her binoculars, she could hardly believe her luck. Her heartbeat quickened as she walked down Marsh Lane, binoculars bouncing gently on her pert breasts. Bird watching covers a multitude of sins, she thought, and here's me, miss goody two shoes who no one would ever suspect on her way to screw the sweetest boy in the village. The thought sent waves of pleasure running through her and her pace quickened.

Marsh Lane led, as its name implied, to the salt marshes and its myriad seabirds. There were only three houses on the lane and Peter's was the last one looking out across a vast expanse of marsh under the huge Norfolk sky. She glanced around her. There was

Sweet and Sour

no one, the other houses were out of sight around the bend. The spring sunshine warmed her as she walked up the drive, her every nerve tingling. The front door stood open to allow the cooling breeze to flow; she went in silently.

Grinning broadly, she slipped off her shoes thinking I'll surprise him, the little tinker. She quietly closed the door and crept upstairs. Peeping around the doorway she took in the sight of him, his head stuck in a girlie magazine. Amelia admired his long slender body from the tousled hair to the tip of his stockinged feet. Oh, what beautiful feet he has. Her gaze moved and dwelt on his slim hips and his trouser bulge, oh, God, that delicious trouser bulge.

Sensing her presence, Peter suddenly looked up, his eyebrows almost disappearing into his hairline 'Bloody hell, Amelia, you startled me. What are you doing here? It's only Thursday, I thought….' His voice trailed off as he saw the raw lust in her cornflower eyes 'Oh, I see' he said as a familiar warmth spread to his groin 'you know about Mum and dad. They won't be back for ages; aunty Beryl is poorly. Nothing is secret for long in this village.'

She leaned insolently on the door jamb, folding her arms under her bosom, a forefinger tapping on her bare arm. An electric thrill buzzed through her from hairline to groin where it found its greatest intensity. She shuddered. Peter was just eighteen with the body of a Greek statue and the stamina of a young stallion.

She decided to tease him 'look at the state of this room Peter, it's a pigsty.' He looked embarrassed but didn't reply. 'Clothes scattered all around, records and books all over your bed, cricket gear and shoes everywhere.' She noticed, too, the huge dollop of seagull droppings smeared across the window. It had been there last Friday and now the sun had dried it into dark brown goo. Ugh, she thought and, turned her attention back to Peter. 'Have you got our play toys?'

He leered, looking her up and down. The summer print dress pinched in at her tiny waist was a little too short for a vicar's wife some might say. Hell, it was 1959 for god's sake, the world was changing. He rose slowly from the divan bed, uncoiling like a sensuous serpent, stretching languidly, knowing the effect he was having on her 'and what if I can't find them?'

'Then I'll have to spank you, naughty boy.'

'Oh, yes please, mistress.'

Removing the bottom drawer from the chest of drawers, he retrieved the riding crop, handcuffs, mask, and blindfold from the floor underneath it.

Amelia crossed to his wardrobe, fingers shaking as she hurriedly shed her clothes. She pulled on his five-sizes-too- big riding boots. The leather felt good on her calves. Marching up to him, her persona changed, her eyes hardened, and her voice became harsh. 'Give me those handcuffs, boy' she barked 'clothes off, now.'

Sweet and Sour

He obeyed meekly, soon standing naked before her. She lifted his penis with the riding crop and inspected its already swelling girth 'I suppose it will have to do' she pointed the crop bedwards and he lay down arms stretched above his head. Amelia smirked as she clipped the handcuffs on and secured him to the bedhead. She blindfolded him before delivering a light, stinging slap to his cheek. She slipped on her bandit mask and three-cornered hat. Tapping him on the scrotum she was rewarded by a soft moan of pleasure. Turning her attention to his nipples, she started to strike, gently at first, but with gradually growing force. He groaned.

Scooping up his feet, she forced them high into the air 'You're a very wicked boy for making me want to fuck you.' The four-letter word felt good on her lips, and she started to spank his buttocks thymically 'fuck, fuck, fuck.' As each stroke landed, she became more and more excited, striking harder and harder, her voice becoming a croak. She felt her juices soaking her thighs as her gorged clitoris forced its way out of its fleshy prison.

'Please, mistress' he moaned 'I'll be a good boy, I promise.' It was the signal that he was ready.

She mounted him then, emitting wild cries of pleasure as she sought her satisfaction, riding him harder and harder, slapping his thigh with her crop, feeling him thrusting powerfully upwards. The sun shone warmly through the window onto her back making her sweat profusely. She climaxed with a shout of joy as the orgasms rolled through her one after another. At long last, she sank, spent, onto his chest, whimpering softly. 'You're a very naughty boy' she whispered in his ear 'and I'll have to punish you again tomorrow.'

After an age, she pushed herself up and removed his blindfold and handcuffs. Smiling into his eyes, she kissed him thrusting her tongue down his throat whilst sliding her hand down his washboard stomach. She grasped his manhood. Oh, God, she thought, so much better than boring bloody Justin and his missionary moves. The thought of her husband's clammy hands on her and the sight of his pallid skin revolted her. Thank God he only pestered her twice a month. She forced her thoughts back to the present finishing her kiss and stepping back.

'Are you not afraid we'll get caught out Amelia? I mean, we seem to be doing it an awful lot lately.'

Her laughter rang confidently 'but we're always so careful, darling Peter. I saw your parents catch the train to King's Lynne. It's an hour's journey. Even if someone saw me leaving here, they'd assume I'd called to see your mother about the church flowers.' She stroked his hair soothingly 'Tomorrow they'll go to your aunt Julia's playing whist, as always.' She brushed his crotch lightly her tongue darting suggestively over her lips 'I'll see you tomorrow my sweet and I promise you an incredibly special treat.'

Sweet and Sour

She thrust her thumb in her mouth, sucking, '*very special.*'

Despite her reassurance and sexy promise, worry still clouded his mind. This was a small village rife with gossip 'what about Justin? Doesn't he suspect anything?'

Her mouth twisted contemptuously 'he thinks I'm out and about in the parish doing good works, or birdwatching on the marshes, he never even asks where I've been the gullible fool.'

Peter frowned 'All the same…'

She slapped his inner thigh then pressed her forefinger across his lips giving him a reproachful look, the last thing she needed was the best sex partner she'd ever had getting cold feet. 'Stop worrying, Peter, everything's all right, we're too careful to get caught. I'm the vicar's wife, remember? The daughter of the bishop. No one would ever suspect me of anything untoward unless you were to confide in anyone, that is.'

'God, Amelia, I couldn't tell anyone. It would ruin you and there's my dad's career at the bank.'

She got up and started collecting her scattered clothes. As she dressed, she couldn't help feeling that the room had changed somehow. She looked around, everything seemed normal. She shrugged and continued to dress; she'd closed the front door so no one could have sneaked in to spy on them. I mustn't let him spook me she thought, I'm thirty, a bright, mature woman with needs. He's my only relief from boring, sermonizing Justin and the endless round of tea and bloody scones with old biddies.

Amelia made her way to her car turning her thoughts to the evening meal. Mr Jackson, the butcher, was crossing her path to his car. 'Good afternoon, Claude, how's your Sheila?'

Jackson looked her boldly in the eye, smirked, and gave her a lewd wink 'not as satisfied as you, I shouldn't wonder, Amelia.' He shook his head and walked away chortling.

Panic gripped Amelia now, Peter had a Saturday job at Jackson's butchers, he must have confided in him. 'You dirty little shit' she cursed 'you bloody horrible little shit, you couldn't resist bragging, eh? Her knees sagged and she stumbled to her car, her mind in turmoil. She was ruined, Justin was ruined. If they ever gave him another parish it would be in some inner-city hellhole on a tiny stipend. What would her father the bishop say? She sat in the car sobbing, tears coursing down her cheeks. How could you do this to me, you stupid little boy? How? Anger started to grow, replacing the sick feeling in her stomach. I'll have it out with you, you slimy little bastard, you're not going to get away with this. Her thoughts were dark as she started the car.

'But Amelia, I wouldn't tell anyone, especially not that old letch Jackson.'

Sweet and Sour

'Liar!' she screamed as she whipped her hand across his face 'There's only you who could have told him, you stupid little bugger.'

His face was puce, and his eyes blazed, he put his hand to the red welt across his cheek 'why are you accusing me, you bitch?' He yelled 'It's more likely to be some other bloke you're screwing' he shouted, 'Just get out of my house, you fucking whore.'

The red mist descended, and her sight blurred 'What?' she screeched. Her hand fell on the cricket bat left carelessly on the dresser 'You arrogant little bastard.' She lashed out, hitting him over the head. He groaned and fell backwards onto the bed his eyes seemed to shift around the room unfocussed.

'Oh, sweet Jesus, what have I done?' she started to shake him 'Peter, Peter are you all right?' her voice was high pitched, she felt on the edge of insanity 'oh, dear God, please help me. What have I done?'

Peter seemed to be looking past her towards the window. He screwed up his eyes to focus then raised his hand weakly, pointing. 'The bird shit's gone' he mumbled, 'window cleaner, second Thursday, every month.' he sank back on the bed.

Amelia turned and looked; the once filthy window was now pristine. That's what had been different about the room. She staggered over and looked down. Yes, there in the flowerbed, two holes made by the window cleaner's ladder. Old man Sillito, the biggest gossip in the village. She stumbled back to the bed and fainted.

When she came to, Amelia was confused, she sat up and looked at Peter 'oh, dear God. She saw at once that he wasn't breathing. There were thin tendrils of blood oozing from his nose and ears. She screamed and ran downstairs to the phone.

'Emergency, which service do you require, please?'

'An ambulance, there's been a terrible accident. Hurry, please.'

She slowly climbed the stairs hoping to be wrong but knowing she wasn't. Crossing to the bed, she lay on top of Peter stroking his hair, stunned beyond tears. 'I'm so sorry my darling, so very, very sorry.'

She heard the ambulance bell ringing, getting louder. She met them at the door arms sagged at her side, eyes lifeless. 'He's up there' she indicated with her head 'first on the right, fractured skull.'

The men ran past her, and she made her way to her car. What now? Police, court case, scandal, life in prison. She started the car and drove to the village where she parked at the edge of the pond. Across the village green, young mothers were pushing prams laughing with each other. Dogs barked and children frolicked. So normal, all so bloody normal. Why did everything still look normal? She couldn't stand it any longer, she started the car and drove off but where to? Where to now?

Sweet and Sour

A blue light flashed behind her; it was constable Goggins signalling her to pull over. Amelia panicked as wild terror gripped her. She pressed the accelerator to the floor the only thought in her head was I must away, she had to escape the unbearable horror she had created. Her car could easily out-pace Goggins battered old police vehicle. Down Sandringham Road she sped, the ringing of the police car bell fading behind her.

As she rounded the bend the warning lights were flashing on the ungated level crossing. The intercity express was due at any moment.

Amelia drove onto the crossing as the thundering locomotive sounded its two-tone warning. She stopped on the line and looked at the oncoming monster whose vibrations shook the car, becoming more intense by the second. The Hee-haw of the Diesel's horn was deafening as, too late, steel shrieked on steel. In that moment she became utterly calm. Applying the handbrake and turning off the ignition would tell them she'd done it deliberately, an act of contrition, a final penance. 'Sorry everyone, sorry God' she whispered and closed her eyes.

Stones of Fire

Agnar of Cynebald, known as Agnar the Angry, glowered at the three captured chieftains kneeling before him, their hands bound behind them.

'You chose to defy me, now your men lay dead, wounded or captured. I will put you to death, of course, but how quickly or slowly depends on you.'

The three hapless prisoners looked Agnar in the eye, puzzled. None was afraid to die but the manner of death for a captured chieftain was always a swift beheading as befitted their rank.

'You can order your men to join my army or refuse and be thrown to starving boars to be eaten alive. The choice is yours.'

Ceolmund of Leofwine, the bravest of the three captives spoke up. 'My men will make their own choice; I will give no order.'

Agnar's lips curled through his greasy beard, his hooked nose and dark, glinting eyes gave him a vulturine presence. He cursed inwardly. A chieftain's order bound his men to allegiance. Agnar needed men to replace those lost in battle and Ceolmund's warriors were the best. All captives were given the

Sweet and Sour

choice of joining him or being sold as slaves. They always chose to join him then a great number deserted.

Ceolmund said 'you intend to attack Queen Hirtha of the Belgae next spring. We have a kinship with her. I'll not bind my men to treachery.'

'Then your fate is sealed Ceolmund.' He turned to a slave 'send for the cart of pigs. Prepare the enclosure.'

Ceolmund spoke calmly 'Hirtha is a powerful sorceress. Many years ago, an invading army perished in a wall of fire she conjured before they got within spear throw.'

Agnar laughed 'A simple trick revealed by my previous soothsayer. Oil was poured into two trenches fifty paces apart the land between also drenched in it. When the invaders reached the second trench both were lit, the ground beneath them then burned. They died like the fools they were. Hirtha is merely a cunning she-wolf.'

Then was Ceolmund put to his horrendous death, his men sent to the slave market for they could not be trusted.

*

Oswald, son Ceolmund, lay on the battlefield where he had been left for dead. The axe that felled him had glanced off his helmet without penetrating it. The attacking warrior had been too busy defending himself to finish him off.

As Oswald slowly regained consciousness, he became aware of gentle rain falling on his face. His head ached abominably, and his thirst raged. He sat up, slowly, painfully, looking around him at the scene of carnage. Dead warriors were strewn far and wide, crows pecking their eyes and tongues, squabbling noisily over the choicest titbits.

Painful memories returned. The defeat of the three tribes was a result of their arrogance. Each leader believed he knew best, refusing to take orders from his father who was the most experienced of them. Agnar had taken advantage of this, driving a wedge between them then encircling three separate pockets. They had fought like wolves, but defeat was inevitable against a well organised Agnar.

Oswald found his sword then staggered to a nearby stream and drank deeply. He was washing the dried blood from his face that he heard a voice in his head. 'Arise, Oswald, go to your kin the Belgae. Take no weapons, cast off regalia of rank, above all be humble.' Oswald reached for his sword without which he felt naked. The voice was insistent 'Would you be like the other fools and take no advice?' Reluctantly he released his hold. 'Who are you?' he asked aloud.

'One who will protect you without need of violence. Now, arise and go.'

Oswald found the voice compelling, and he had nowhere else to go. He threw away his weapons, stripped low ranking warrior's a corpse and donned its clothes.

*

In her large roundhouse, Queen Hirtha sat cross-legged on a bearskin. Her eyes were closed, her back erect, next to her sat her daughter Joscelyne in a similar pose. They were in deep meditation, the central fire bathing them in a flickering glow. After an hour both stirred, opening their eyes. The Queen clapped her hands and a servant brought two cups of warm mead.

'You saw what I saw Joscelyne? Agnar will come next year, and he is powerful.'

'The spring will be wet, mother, his oxcarts will sink, he'll be delayed.'

'We must plan our defence daughter.'

'What are we to do mother?' Joscelyne asked, her dark eyes serious, her brow creased 'he has a huge army.'

Hirtha brushed her long black locks from her pallid face, 'I shall sleep child and when I awake, I will know.'

The next morning Hirtha awoke and went to her daughter's bed, 'arise, daughter, I have news.'

Joscelyne looked into Hirtha's deep dark eyes. This morning they shone and were flecked with gold, a sign her mother was about to make a prophecy. 'News, mother?'

'A young prince comes; he will be your husband should he prove worthy and should you accept him.'

This news filled Joscelyne with a thrill of delight. For some time now she had been gazing at young men of the tribe, feelings of womanhood stirring her loins. But her joy was tempered with anxiety. 'This is wonderful news, mother, but what of Agnar?'

'We have to build a temple of stone to focus the power and spirit of our tribe if we are not to be conquered.'

'But we have not the time, surely?'

'Nothing is impossible with magic my child.'

Joycelene accepted her mother's answer for she knew of her great powers. Her thoughts returned to the young prince.

'And what of my husband, mother?' Jocelyne asked excitedly 'I shall be fifteen summers at the solstice; I have had twelve blood moons and still no husband.' Her face sagged to a sulk 'most women are married by my age.'

Hirtha brushed her daughter's cheek and kissed her forehead tenderly. 'Most women of your age are not future queens, Joscelyne. The right soul must be sought.'

*

Oswald's head ached fiercely, each stride jolted, every path seemed fraught with obstacles, a rocky outcrop to be climbed here, a bog to be avoided there. He was ravenously hungry and at a loss what to do

Sweet and Sour

when he came upon a hut on the edge of a wood. He called out, believing it to be the dwelling of a peasant. The door was flung open and a hunting party of a tribe he didn't know surrounded him, spears pointing.

The leader, a large man in a bearskin robe, addressed him.

'Who are you, what is your business here?'

'He is a thief come to steal' cried one of the men, 'kill him.'

Oswald bowed 'I am no thief good sirs but a mere traveller seeking his kin the Belgae.'

The man who called him a thief screamed 'liar! I say kill him.'

The leader held up his hand for silence. 'I have yet to see an unarmed thief. You dress as a warrior yet carry no weapons, why is this?'

'Because I wish no harm to any, sir, but merely to visit my kin.' He told of the battle with Agnar but not of the voice.

'Any enemy of Agnar is welcome here, come, eat with us.'

After the meal, the leader told him 'Though you are a warrior, yet you are humble. You took a great risk by carrying no weapons. It proved your honest intent. Had you been armed or arrogant I would have slain you.'

Oswald thanked the head huntsman and went on his way but still met many obstacles. And now a swollen stream flowed before him.

The old woman sat in the rain dressed in rags, her scrawny arms outstretched in supplication 'Oh, fine young warrior please, I beg of you, help me to the other side.'

Oswald saw one of her eyes was opaque the other dull. She smelled like a pigpen.

'I have no time old mother.'

'Noble sir,' she pleaded 'my husband of forty summers lies dying, I must go to him. Please, I beg, help me.'

Oswald sighed and relented, hoisting the woman onto his back. As he ploughed into the stream, she dug her long nails into his flesh and started screaming in terror.

'Be calm mother, for I am strong, and you are safe.'

Once across, the old woman began wailing 'Oh, my cat, I have forgotten my cat, please, sir, we must go back.'

'No, I must go, be off to your husband, crone.'

Her face was a mask of misery as she pleaded 'do you not have a grandmother, young sir? Was she me, would your treatment be such? My cat is ancient, she will perish alone.'

A picture of his late, beloved grandmother came to mind, she, too, had loved cats. He groaned, 'very well, I will go back and look for it.'

'That will avail nought sir, she will not come to strangers.'

Sweet and Sour

Oswald clapped his hand to his forehead, 'the gods punish me this day' he said and lifted her again. They re-crossed the icy water, the old woman emitted ear-piercing shrieks. Oswald felt like weeping. 'Why me?' he called to the heavens, 'what have I done?'

They reached the bank and the old woman scurried way to a clump of shrubs calling her cat. Thunder and lightning crashed and flashed through the pouring rain as the woman continued to call, oblivious of the storm. After ten long minutes, the scrawny black animal crept from its hiding place to be scooped up by the woman. She returned to Oswald her good eye glowing with gratitude. 'May the gods reward you, young sir.'

'The reward I crave, woman, is to have thee at peace as we cross back and thy fingernails not piercing my flesh.'

'It shall be so, sir.'

And peaceful she was, but the cat climbed onto his head digging in its claws deep into his scalp and screeched its fear of the raging waters. Oswald wept. 'Why?' he cried to the heavens, 'is the sacrifice of my father not enough?'

Reaching the far bank once more, he placed the old lady down gently as the cat leapt off his head and slunk away. She clung to him smiling, her thin lips drawn back over her few remaining blackened stumps, her breath as rank as a dung pile. 'I have a reward for you, young warrior' she said and took an amulet from around her neck. 'It is made from the metal that falls from the heavens; it always points to the North so you will never be lost.' Tears flooded the creases of her face, 'it would please me greatly if you wore it always.'

Oswald's frustration evaporated like dawn mist, he felt deeply humbled. The amulet must be the only thing of value she had ever possessed. She placed it in his hand, and he allowed her to close his fingers over it. It was heavy, silver-grey and roughly in the shape of a star, having jagged but not sharp edges. It felt warm. He bowed 'thank you, good mother, you are most generous' he said, his voice cracking. He bent and kissed her forehead, 'now, I must take my leave for it grows late and I have far to go.'

He turned and hurried away; he had not gone ten paces when he heard her say 'go in peace Oswald the Great of the Belgae.'

Shocked, Oswald spun on his heel. The old woman had vanished.

*

'Call the council Joscelyne, have them attend me now.'

The three men and three women assembled, Hirtha described the temple, the type of stone required and the date for completion.

A stunned silence followed then Willa, the healer, spoke. 'Great Queen, the stone you require lies four leagues distant. Cutting and carting it would take years, not months.'

Hirtha smiled, her face radiant. She extended her hands palms up. The council rose from their places and floated. 'Have faith, my dear lady Willa, the stones will cut like mud, they will weigh nothing.' She lowered the startled council.

'A young prince arrives tomorrow dressed as a common warrior. If he and Joscelyne are willing, they will wed, followed by three days of feasting. Afterwards, shall our sacred work commence.'

The council nodded solemnly, then Hirtha dismissed them to spread the word among their people.

*

Approaching the Belgae village, Oswald was surprised to sees there were no sentries, nor did the dogs bark at him. There was an ethereal atmosphere about the place, and he felt a deep sense of peace. People smiled and waved greetings as he passed by. A boy pointed to Hirtha's house waving him towards it, then ran ahead to bring the news of his arrival.

Hirtha herself welcomed Oswald and introduced him to Joscelyne. The very air seemed to crackle between them as they eyed each other admiringly. A meal followed then Oswald was shown to the bachelor quarters.

'Did you not find him handsome, daughter?' Hirtha asked.

'Handsome? No, mother, not handsome, he is beautiful. '

'I tested him sorely on his journey. He is strong, sensible and compassionate. He will rule with you after my time if you will have each other.'

'I could cast a spell on him mother…'

'No!' that is not the purpose of magic, and you know it Joscelyne.'

Joseline's cheeks flushed 'sorry mother.'

Hirtha's anger melted 'I saw the way you two looked at each other my daughter, you will have no need of spells.'

The next morning, at dawn, Oswald was surprised to see families sitting in circles, their eyes closed, chanting. He felt a warm vibration emanate from them running through him like the joyful current of life itself.

Over breakfast, Oswald asked the bachelors about their laws and customs, not wanting to cause embarrassment. They told him their only law was: If it harms no other, do what thou wilt shall be the whole of the law. They were friendly, but Oswald felt uncomfortable among them. 'Where are your swords, your shields, war axes, spears?' he asked, 'how do you defend yourselves?'

A frail young man stepped forward 'My name is Bloewold' he said, 'strike me.' When Oswald refused, he said 'please, *try* to strike me, I will not harm you,

Sweet and Sour

Oswald, I promise.' The others laughed and Oswald's face burned, how dare these non-warriors scorn him.

He threw a punch. The blow stopped six inches from Bloewald's face as if it had hit a solid pillow. He struck again with the same result. Frustrated, he kicked out. Bloewold smiled and jerked his hand forward an inch. Oswald was propelled backwards by an unseen force. He sat down sharply, bemused.

'What sorcery is this?' What evil do you practice here?'

Bloewold helped him up, smiling. 'No sorcery, Oswald, just our focussed life force. We are the protectors.' They explained the only weapons they needed were for hunting. 'We do not steal or lie, and trade fairly will all.' The others muttered agreement. 'We give others no reason for resentment.' Bloewold smiled and bowed. 'If you stay, you will come to see the wisdom of our ways.'

Later, Oswald was summoned before the Queen and Joscelyne who took his hand. A great wave of love surged through him as he gazed into her molten brown eyes.

'My Lord Oswald of Leofwine, will you be my husband? Will you take me this day before my tribe and prove me a worthy successor to my mother?'

Oswald felt his heart leap for joy the love that consumed him was pure, never had anything in his life felt so right. 'I will, my noble lady, gladly, I will.'

Among the other tribes, it was the bride's father who made the marriage match, this was alien to him, yet Hirtha stood by radiating joy.

That night at sunset they took their vows before the altar stone which was spread with a white sheet. Hirtha officiated. Then she stripped them naked to cries of appreciation from the tribe.

'You must lay her upon the altar and consummate the marriage, all must witness the match is pure.'

Oswald was shy until Joscelyne took his hand and whispered, 'it is our custom my Lord, all here love you, be not embarrassed.'

When it was done, Hirtha raised the sheet high crying 'behold, the virgin blood.'

The tribe responded, shouting 'the union is pure, long live this sacred union.'

There followed three days of feasting, dancing and merriment yet none got drunk. Oswald was amazed.

*

After three days of hard marching, they reached the stones. Ninety men and ninety women with chisels, ropes and hammers. Hirtha muttered an incantation and drew the shapes she required on the stone with charcoal, then drew her forefinger down the lines. 'Now, cut where I have drawn.' They found the stone where they cut was as soft as clay yet an inch from their chisels it was solid. The cutting took only four days.

Sweet and Sour

On the fifth day, Hirtha raised the stones. 'Tie your ropes about them and pull' she ordered. And so, five days later, they returned to the village.

For the next month, Hirtha studied the stars making calculations, then drew her plan with charcoal on a scraped goatskin. She gave it to Oswald who oversaw the digging of the foundations. After another month, the work was completed.

Now Hirtha turned her attention to the defeat of her enemies. She made strange requests of her people. They did not understand but they did what she asked without question. A furnace was built with great bellows which Hirtha filled with sand and from which a strange new material poured which she moulded into iridescent spheres. She sent two carts to the sea tribes and bought huge quantities of salt, which she stored in an empty granary.

Hirtha had all the mead collected and had them boil it, turning the vapour back into liquid on large sheets of copper, collecting it in jars.

Hirtha's outward appearance was always serene but deep inside she worried. The Belgae numbered a mere two thousand. Agnar's army was three times that size. Agnar had a magician, a man of the dark arts whose skill as a seer she had heard much. Yet her people were unafraid for their faith in their queen was unshakable. She prayed their faith was well-founded.

*

Agnar sent for Daeldrik. 'Look into your scrying vessel, soothsayer' he ordered 'what does the witch plan.'

Daeldrik took a shallow highly polished silver bowl from his robes and poured water into it from a silver flask then sprinkled in a dark powder. Purple clouds swirled and billowed as he stared. 'I can see a great temple my lord built of stone.'

'Impossible, you are wrong. My spies of two months ago reported no such structure.'

'Daeldrik bowed low and remained silent. It did not pay to contradict Agnar.

'What do you see of our victory, Daeldrik? Speak truly.'

'I do see victory, my Lord, but it will be much delayed, for there will be floods.'

Agnar snorted as he tugged his beard, this meant waiting in his captured villages. Men would become bored and desert. He would capture a few and have them roasted on a spit to discourage others. Still, it was a waste of warriors. He brushed these thoughts aside. 'What attack date is most auspicious?'

Again, Daeldrik pored over the bowl, then breathed a relieved sigh. 'The solstice, my Lord.

'Ah, yes, the pagans will be celebrating and unprepared. I am pleased Daeldrik.'

'You have nought to fear Great Agnar' Daeldrik enthused, 'they are unarmed save for hunting weapons and small daggers they use as tools. Their Queen has

Sweet and Sour

much silver and gold, their crops are plentiful, their animals are fat. Their women and children are lithe and the men healthy. They will command high prices as slaves.'

Agnar paused, stroking his beard; this was too easy. One thing he had learned was that no battle was ever easy. All sprang their own surprises and evil spirits lurked to trap the unwary. 'Send out spies Daeldrik, see what preparations she makes.'

The spies returned, reporting that a great stone temple had been built surrounded by a ditch. They had captured a young goatherd and tortured him. He revealed the temple was built using great magic. 'We slit his throat sire and stole his clothes and some goats to make it look like the work of brigands.'

Agnar was worried, a great stone temple? So, Daeldrik was right. How could this have been done? He sent for Daeldrik again. The soothsayer gazed into his scrying bowl, this time he saw nothing, and he knew Hirtha was blocking him. The spies had been a bad idea.

Daeldrik dare not admit he saw nothing. His predecessor had met a terrible end being slowly impaled on a stake through his anus. 'I still foretell a great victory, mighty Agnar. First, you must surround them then attack with the rising sun at your back.'

Agnar spat and struck Daeldrik's face with the flat of his hand, 'impudent cur, do not lecture me on battle tactics.' But inwardly Agnar was planning just that.

*

On solstice eve Agnar's army was in position. He was impressed by the temple and by the quality of the village buildings. He instructed his commanders not to burn the village nor kill anyone who could be sold. He called Daeldrik to his side. 'Look again soothsayer what is the purpose of this structure?'

Daedric needed no scrying bowl for he could sense a vortex of power surrounding the temple. 'It is a place of worship and sacrifice, my Lord, there is great power here.'

'And are her powers greater than yours?'

Deadrick clenched his fists inside his robe to stop the trembling he felt was about to betray his fear. 'No, my Lord' he lied. To admit the truth would be to invite disaster.

'Then we attack at the first light before the sun rises.'

*

Hirtha ordered her people to pour the salt into the ditch around the temple. That done, she had her glass spheres filled with the mead spirit and given to the defenders. She called a council of war and gave instructions.

Two hours before dawn Hirtha sat on the altar stone facing east, on her right Joscelyne, on her left Oswald. before them sat the tribal elders. Within the temple sat the entire tribe, except for the defenders

Sweet and Sour

who were spaced around the out ditch. All were quietly chanting.

Agnar's men surrounded the village, all were eager for plunder and rape, their weapons newly sharpened.

As grey streaks lit the horizon a horn sounded.

They charged.

Around the ditch, the protectors raised their hands and with a mighty shout thrust them forward. From the salt in the ditch sprang a wall of blue fire. Agnar's front warriors stopped but the ones behind them pressed forward thrusting the front men into the flames where they died screaming.

Behind the protectors, women threw the spheres the Queen had made high over their enemies where they burst. A rain of droplets cascaded down. The women then threw torches and the liquid exploded. Warriors screamed in their death throes as purple flames raged. The raiders now withdrew filled with awe. Fighting they knew but magic terrified them.

Agnar flew into a rage and ordered his men to charge again.

Inside the village, the spheres were all used up and the protectors were tiring but the defence held once more.

Agnar now concentrated his men on the East side their backs to the glowing sky.

'I shall make a breach in the fire Lord Agnar' said Daeldrik 'once through if you slay the witch all this will vanish. He chanted an incantation his hands thrust before him.

The breach appeared and Agnar's men surged forward. Oswald grabbed a spear and ran forward defending the breach with a ferocity that surprised his enemies. Only two at a time could fit the breach and Oswald slew two score men before the rest retreated. They cried to Agnar fearfully that there was great magic at work, that Oswald was protected by evil spirits and could not be killed.

Hirtha called loudly 'Withdraw or die, Agnar, for you are defeated.'

'A great victory, you said, Daeldrik., but you never said for whom.' He struck the soothsayer a fatal blow 'so die traitors.'

Agnar took up three spears, three people would not live to enjoy their victory. He ran towards the breach and the twin pillars through which Hirtha sat on the altar stone. He threw his spears with great speed and accuracy. The first sped towards Hirtha who waved her hand and deflected it. The second flew at Jocelyne's heart. She raised a finger and it fell to earth. The third spear flashed into Oswald's chest where it struck the amulet and shattered to dust. Agnar drew his sword and ran screaming his battle cry.

As Agnar reached the alter the sun broke the horizon, its light reflecting from Hirtha's eyes grew in intensity as she focused on her enemy. The peoples'

Sweet and Sour

chanting rose in intensity and Agnar spun in a vortex of power. His robes caught fire and he shrieked and writhed in his death agony, still trying to reach his nemesis. Hirtha's power held him up and kept him alive, burning, inflicting upon him the agonies he had so readily inflicted upon others. When at last the sun cleared the horizon Hirtha closed her eyes. Agnar fell in ashes.

Oswald felt Hirtha's trembling hand upon his arm. 'Please, my lord, carry me home, for I am spent.'

Looking at Hirtha, Oswald saw that she had aged greatly, and he recognised the old woman he had carried over the stream.

'Great magic requires a great sacrifice of the spirit 'she said 'and I have given all I have.'

Laying on her bed, Hirtha beckoned Joscelyne and Oswald near. 'My time has come, my children. I leave you to rule the people wisely and with compassion.'

'But mother' Joscelyne cried, we do not have your power, we cannot hope to match you.'

'Your powers will grow, Joscelyne, rule wisely aided by your strong prince.'

Oswald took her hand 'is there ought we can do for you great queen?'

'You can tell our story down the ages, Oswald. Let our mighty temple stand on this, the Plain of Salis, forever and henceforth let it be known as The Great Henge of Stone.

Nobody's Prize

Ronald stooped to his son, 'mummy has been very naughty, Archie, she went with another man, and now she wants to take you away from me, you, my only son.'

Archie sobbed and a tear started down his cheek, he didn't understand why his daddy was so angry. Had he been naughty? He reached up to his father's arms and felt himself being lifted into the warm security of daddy's chest. He was enveloped in strong arms that squeezed a little too tightly. He burst into a torrent of tears as the misery of the last few weeks poured out of him.

The first three and a half years of Archie's life had been blissful and carefree but then tensions had started to creep into his life. His parents' voices had changed from loving and gentle to harsh and loud, with long silences in between. Both made comments to him that he could not understand 'Your father's a two-timing no-good son-of-a-bitch' his mother had said just that morning. Archie couldn't understand, he only knew that it was something bad.

Ronald and Angela Beddows were splitting up. Ronald had had numerous affairs and Angela had slept with her office manager for revenge. It was a

Sweet and Sour

small office and, as Ronald worked for the same company, the affair was soon discovered.

The front door clicked open then closed with a bang, Angela came into the lounge. Ronald turned to see her standing very still, her face pinched and pale. She stared at him balefully, fists clenched at her sides 'And if you're thinking of getting custody of *my* son, or even visiting rights, you bastard, think again.' Her face twisted into a snarl, eyes narrowing to hate-filled slits 'with your record of infidelity, you won't stand a chance.'

Archie felt his father's grip tighten, it was hurting now, and he howled his protest. Ronald ignored his son's wriggling, too wrapped up in his problems. 'See what you've done now? You've upset him with your nastiness, bitch.' He glared at her long and hard before finally realising he was holding his son too tightly. He eased his grip and kissed the boy on the forehead 'sorry little man' he whispered in his ear.

'Give him to me you clueless bugger' she snapped and quickly closed the distance between them, grabbing Archie firmly and wrenching him away. Ronald let go to avoid hurting the boy.

Archie's screams rose even higher in his distress, everything he knew that was safe and loving was being torn away by the two people he loved with all his four-year-old heart. His misery knew no bounds, what had he done to make mummy and daddy fight?

After Archie was put to bed Ronald and Angela sat in their living room in icy silence, each staring disinterestedly at the TV. Finally, Ronald could stand the atmosphere no longer 'I'm off to the pub for an hour.'

'Got a new barmaid that needs screwing, have they?'

'Piss off, bitch.'

The front door slammed, Angela sighed and went to the drink's cabinet, pouring herself a large gin and tonic. 'Bastard' she muttered 'if he thinks he's getting my son, he's dead wrong.'

At eleven-thirty Ronald staggered into the living room to find Angela on her i-pad. His lips curled downwards in a sarcastic sneer 'checking out the talent, are you? Looking for some other poor sod to foist yourself onto' he slurred?

She threw the i-pad at him 'I was looking at childrens' clothes if you must know, not that you'd care if my son went bare-arsed.'

'*Our* son, bitch. If you think you can stop me from having joint custody, forget it.'

Their voices rose as the argument raged; upstairs, Archie awoke. The little boy lay silently weeping, listening to his parents fighting. He heard his name being shouted; he must have been very naughty. He couldn't think of what he'd done, but he knew it must be all his fault that's why his name was being shouted. Then he heard the thuds and his mother's

Sweet and Sour

screams as his father started punching her. Archie climbed out of bed and, taking Fuzzy his teddy bear, crept downstairs.

They didn't notice him as entered the lounge clutching Fuzzy to his chest, fat tears rolling down his crumpled cheeks. 'Please stop' he pleaded 'please, daddy, stop. Hit me and Fuzzy, not my mummy.' he walked between them facing his father's anger. He held up his Teddy bear 'please, daddy, hit me and Fuzzy, not my mummy.'

They fell into shocked silence, Ronald, dropped to his knees before the little boy. 'Oh, dear Christ! What have I done to you, my poor little man? Daddy is so, so sorry.'

Angela wiped the tears from her bruised cheeks then scooped Archie up and hurried him back upstairs. 'I'm so sorry Archie, darling' she said, 'mummy and daddy have been very silly, sweetheart. We'll stop shouting now, I promise.'

Archie's large blue eyes were filled with tearful confusion and his lips trembled 'Have I been a naughty boy, mummy?'

Tears streamed down Angela's face as guilt pangs pierced her heart, the full enormity of what they were doing to Archie crashed into her consciousness with brutal force. She sniffled, trying to calm herself. 'No, darling, you've been a good boy, it's because mummy and daddy don't love each other anymore and we want to live apart. We were fighting over you. Who would you like to live with, darling, me or daddy?' It was an impossible question to ask a four-and-a-half-year-old.

'I want to live at Grandma's house, mummy. Grandma doesn't shout. Grandma lets me eat lots of cake.'

'But Grandma lives a long way away, Archie, remember? We went on the train?'

'Can we go to Grandma on the train in the morning mummy?'

'No, Archie, but soon, darling, soon.'

In the morning Archie was dropped at day nursery where he tried to play with the other children, but his heart wasn't in it. He sat on a chair in the corner feeling miserable until Sandra, his favourite nursery nurse, came and asked him what was wrong.

Archie hadn't the words to tell her how he felt so he just mumbled 'daddy hit my mummy.'

Sandra knew of the hostility between Archie's parents. Her gentle heart ached as she picked the little boy up, hugging him to her breast. Archie clung to her, his tiny arms tight around her neck, sniffling miserably. Sandra had seen this sort of thing before. Two adults using their children as the emotional rope and the prize in a marital tug-o'-war. It always had a terrible effect on the children. Children were not the tools of vengeance nor prizes to be won.

*

Sweet and Sour

The next night in the Beddow's house was a repeat of the night before, both were drunk this time. Both yelled their frustrations at one another. Archie lay sobbing in his bed thinking of Grandma. Grandma was always kind, always smiling. No one fought at Grandma's house, and she cuddled him and gave him cake and sweets. He made his mind up, he would go to Grandma, she would make it all better.

In the pre-dawn light, Archie awoke and went to his mother's room 'I'm going to see grandma, mummy.'

Angela, groggy from drink and half asleep said 'OK, darling, you go back to bed, we'll go to see her soon.'

Archie turned and went to his father's room 'Daddy, I'm going to grandma's house on the train.' His father grunted and turned over. Archie stood thinking for a while. Mummy had said it cost a lot of money to go on the train. His father's wallet was on the nightstand. Archie opened it and took a twenty-pound note. He'd give the train people the money and they would take him to grandma's house.

Archie went to his room and took his little suitcase from under his bed. He packed some clean pajamas, socks, underpants, and his favourite Whinny the Pooh T-shirt. Next, he went to the kitchen and made a clumsy jam sandwich which he placed unwrapped in the suitcase. 'It's a long way to Grandma's house, and we might get hungry, Fuzzy' he told his bear. Back in his room, he got dressed feeling proud that he could tie his shoelaces all by himself. 'Come on Fuzzy, we're going to grandma's house.'

Downstairs Archie dragged a chair from the dining room and climbed on it to open the front door.

Outside, on the empty street, Archie met his first problem, he didn't know where the station was. Mummy had taken him in a Taxi. 'I don't know where taxis come from, Fuzzy.'

He stood at the street corner pondering this until he remembered that he knew where the railway line was, it was only at the bottom of the next street. 'If we walk down the railway line, Fuzzy, we'll find the station then we'll give them the money and they'll take us to Grandma's.'

He set off, a deeply troubled little boy, carrying his tiny suitcase, his teddy bear under his arm, determined to go to his grandmother.

He found a hole that older children had made in the railway fence and squeezed through. The deserted line gleamed in the morning light seeming to stretch away forever. Above him in a nearby tree, a blackbird was greeting the new day, the joyful sound made him feel happy. This was a great adventure; he was on his way to Grandma's, and she would make everything better.

When he reached the line, Archie wasn't sure which way to go so he turned to face the rising sun

Sweet and Sour

and started walking. 'There are lots of stations, Fuzzy, we'll find one soon, then we'll eat our sandwich.'

A cool draught from the open front door woke Angela. A feeling that something was wrong engulfed her and rose quickly. Archie's room told its own story. She saw the open drawers the contents hanging haphazardly from them.

She ran downstairs to see the front door yawning open, the chair beside it confirming her fears. 'Wake up Ronald, Archie's gone' she screamed. Throwing a coat over her nightdress, she dashed into the street not waiting for her husband.

Upstairs, Ronald came awake with a start, 'What the hell?' He pushed his legs into his jeans and shoved his feet into his trainers. A quick look in Archie's room then he dashed after his wife. They ran desperately up and down the street calling their son's name. An elderly man walking his dog was questioned. 'Strange,' he said scratching the back of his head, 'I think I saw a child turning down Railway Terrace, I thought it looked odd, but I was too far away to see properly.' He tapped his spectacles 'eye's not too good these days.'

Horror flashed on their faces, and they ran off without a word.

*

Archie turned as he heard a train coming, it was a long way off but seemed to be going amazingly fast. 'I'll show Mr train man our money, Fuzzy, then they'll stop and take us to grandma.' Archie put his suitcase down and pulled the banknote from his pocket. He tucked Fuzzy higher under his arm and waved his banknote. 'Please stop, Mr train, me and Fuzzy want to go to grandma's house.'

Hurtling into the rising sun at ninety miles per hour the driver of the intercity express peered through his bug-smeared windscreen, his attention drawn to the people sprinting down the trackside arms waving, looking panic-stricken. Then he saw the tiny figure waving at him. 'Nooo!' he screamed and slammed on the emergency brakes.

Archie stood rooted to the spot, mesmerized by the oncoming juggernaut thundering towards him. His voice trembled. 'Please Mr train…' The horn blared and sparks flew from the shrieking wheels as they bit the rails.

Ronald and Angela screamed in horror as the engine smashed the life from Archie, hurling his shattered little body forty metres down the track.

He was nobody's prize now.

Skulduggery

I am not a nice man, I'm mean, cunning and ruthless, that's why I survive. Nice people quickly become dead people in my game.

Belfast 1976

In the target, I waited patiently. The shallow curtained alcove behind the counter that concealed me was cramped and claustrophobic. My feet and legs ached from three hours of standing. My nostrils itched from the dust in the air, but I resisted the urge to scratch. The curtain was a scant two inches from my chest; I couldn't risk moving it even slightly. I knew they were watching, waiting, they'd only come once they were certain all was well.

'Get there an hour or so before their team arrive, Jack, that should be time enough. I suggest covert entry from the rear, the back door has only an old mortise lock.'

Frank had briefed me in his laid-back, understated manner, anyone would think this was a run of the mill surveillance job, not a mission to kill two people.

'There'll be a driver and a minder with the bomber, all will be armed' he paused, glancing at his notes, 'once inside, the minder will stand at the door watching the street whilst the bomber is working if things follow the usual pattern. The driver will disappear until collection time. They don't like risking him being spotted hanging around outside the target. That should give you plenty of time to do the job and get clear. OK so far?'

'Fine.'

'Apparently, it doesn't take long to set the bomb so don't hang around once they're inside and the driver has left.'

Frank looked ill at ease, which wasn't like Frank 'I cannot stress enough the importance of placing your shots accurately, understood, Jack?'

I nodded 'Of course, Frank.'

He glanced at his watch 'their Estimated Time of Arrival is oh two-thirty hours, but they are seldom punctual, so you might have a bit of a wait on your hands.'

He paused, scratching his ear, looking shifty, that was another first for Frank. 'Now for the bad news: The intel we have says they are very cagey about this job. They'll scour the whole area before they approach so that means no backup, OK? If they suspect the smallest thing is wrong, they'll abort, and God knows if we'll ever get another chance. So, sorry Jack, but this is a solo mission.'

Frank looked far from sorry, if I got the job done, I could fry in hell directly afterwards for all he cared. The bastard treated me like shit. He was an Eton educated, Brigade of Guards, aristocrat. I was a Barnardo's brat, an orphan, an expendable commodity. If I got killed not many would miss me.

Frank had never shown even a glimmer of embarrassment in previous briefings. Strange, I thought.

'Anything else I should know, Frank? Anything at all?'

'That's all, Jack, so go and get whatever you need. I'll leave the rest to you. You know what to do.'

Anyone who didn't know Frank well would never have noticed his eye contact was not quite the same as it normally was. I couldn't put my finger on what was different. Was Frank holding something back or was it paranoia on my part? Why would he hold anything back? It didn't make sense. I pushed the thought out of my mind and concentrated on the floor plan of the target committing it to memory.

*

I arrived four hours before the ETA. I checked the place and surrounding area out carefully before deciding to enter. The back yard was enclosed by a crumbling seven-foot-high brick wall, the gate sagged open on broken hinges.

The yard was full of rubbish the neighbours had dumped there, forcing me to step gingerly. A dilapidated washing machine, parts of old bicycles plus the heaps of other junk were a real noise hazard. I negotiated this carefully, fearful of alerting others to my presence.

My picks made short work of the old mortise lock. The shop had been empty for months now; the last tenant hadn't even bothered to throw the bolt. There was nothing to steal anyway.

Sliding quietly inside, I crouched motionless against the wall, smelling the stale damp odour of dereliction. I listened intently for full two minutes. I heard nothing except the faint buzzing of traffic up on the main road. I relocked the door then checked out every inch of the place from attic to cellar moving slowly, quietly, disturbing nothing.

Too many of my predecessors had walked into an ambush trusting duff intelligence. Not this soldier, check and recheck.

I found a handprint in the dust on the polished mahogany shop counter. My masked torch showed fresh dust had not yet begun to settle back into it. So, they'd been and checked the place out very recently. A good sign, that.

I thought carefully before choosing my hiding place. The curtained alcove behind the counter had shelves that were only resting on their supports. I removed these and hid them under the counter. The odds were they would have looked in here seen the shelves and dismissed it as a possible hiding place, though that was far from certain.

Sweet and Sour

I watched through the small gap at the curtain's edge where it didn't quite meet the wall. This allowed me a view of the glass door, half of the shop window and the street beyond. I would have a clear shot at the minder when he took up his position. I settled my mind into meditation mode.

An hour before the ETA, a man came into the shop through the front door using a key. He stood in the doorway shining a powerful torch around the walls. I thumbed off the safety catch and held my breath, my heart pounding. The guy went into the back and rattled the door handle vigorously then he went up the stairs, his footsteps echoing in the empty space. He came back down quickly and descended into the cellar. He was back again in a moment.

Returning to the front door, he turned and shone the torch around the walls again, dwelling on my hiding place for what seemed an eternity. The whole of the alcove was lit as bright as day, the thin curtain offering a scant barrier to the probing light. God, I felt exposed, as though the guy must be able to see right through it, though logic dictated otherwise.

I held my breath, listening for a gun being cocked, poised to rip the curtain aside and start shooting.

The man switched off the torch turned and left, locking the door behind him. I breathed out releasing the tension.

I watched as the guy crossed the street and took up position in a darkened doorway. I couldn't see him but knew he'd be watching for any unusual activity.

That there would also be someone in the alley behind the shop I didn't doubt. Stay alert Jack, I told myself, they'll be coming soon.

Yet my mind went back to the briefing, running over it again, evaluating every nuance, every gesture of Frank's. My suspicion that Frank had held something back returned like an itch I couldn't scratch. My instinct said there was definitely something he had not told me, but what? But why? Surely, Frank wouldn't fuck me about on a job this important?

"Deadly" Declan Dooley was Libyan trained and had set booby-trapped bombs that had so far taken the lives of three highly skilled bomb disposal officers as well as many innocent civilians. We knew the shop was only a secondary target, their real aim was to kill a highly trained bomb disposal officer.

Dooley was not a local man, he came to The North when sent for, used his expertise and was spirited away again to safety. He was one of the Provisional Irish Republican Army's greatest assets and they wouldn't risk him unduly. If he hadn't been shagging some top PIRA commander's wife, I wouldn't be waiting for him now.

Intelligence knew almost nothing about Dooley, they had no photos, his age and description were also unknown. Only his lethal work bore his unmistakable signature.

Another hour dragged by before I was alerted by a movement across the street. The man emerged from the doorway and moved off.

Ten minutes later a car drew up at the shop and three people got out. It was too late to worry about the briefing now. Taking great care not to move the curtain, I slowly drew my pistol.

A massive man got out of the car first, the gun looking tiny in his huge fist. He looked up and down the empty street then opened the car boot. The driver was the watcher I'd seen earlier. He came and unlocked the shop door. All three then started carrying sacks into the shop. No one spoke. After five sacks were carried in the driver jumped in the car and drove off. The smell of diesel on fertilizer reached my nostrils and I almost sneezed. The hairs on my neck were tingling.

The smallest of the trio, a slim silhouetted figure carrying a briefcase, shuffled forward clad in a baggy boiler suit and black beanie hat and knelt by the sacks out of my sight, below the counter level.

I heard the click-clack of locks springing as the briefcase was opened. The bomber's torch cast a faint glow, causing ghost-like shadows on the ceiling. It would be enough light to do my business.

Then the minder, instead of guarding the door, started prowling around the sales floor, opening cupboards and kicking at empty cardboard boxes. Christ, I thought, what's he doing? This was not supposed to be happening. He should be standing at the door watching the street where I could get a clear shot at him, not mooching about the shop. I couldn't risk exposing myself and hoping to place my shots with the precision the job demanded.

Things were rapidly turning shit shaped. The bomber wouldn't take long and then the driver would be back. I didn't want a gunfight. This was supposed to be a double execution, not the OK Corral.

Happenings like these are known as the 'buggeration factor' in Army-speak. Nearly every job had one when things went off plan. This was buggeration big time.

Then the minder came behind the counter. I checked my breathing. Had I been stitched up? Fuckin' Frank, have you stitched me up? Where was this guy's pistol pointing? Was it pointing to his front ready to fire the instant he saw me? I heard him pulling out the old-fashioned cash drawer. What the hell did he expect to find in there, for god's sake? But at least this told me he didn't know of my presence. My hand tightened on the pistol grip. His shoe scraped as he swivelled to the alcove and the curtain was jerked aside.

A huge jowly face stared down at me in shocked disbelief, his weapon pointing ceiling-wards Hollywood style. The guy recovered fast and started to bring his gun to bear, but he was way too late. I rammed my pistol into his throat and fired. The plop of the suppressor, though quiet, sounded like a thunderclap to me. The big man's eyes instantly went blank, his face sagged as he flopped, his weapon clattering on the floor. Quickly stepping over the corpse, I leaned over the counter weapon pointing.

'Don't shoot. I surrender. You wouldn't shoot an unarmed woman, would you?' the tiniest of pauses then: 'I'm pregnant.' Her voice came with a heavy Dublin accent, urgent but not panicky.

Declan was a woman? I was stunned and, momentarily taken aback, I hesitated for a second.

As she rose swiftly to her feet it looked for an instant like she was putting her hands up. Then her torch arced into my eyes and her right hand flashed into her pocket. I had adjusted my point of aim as she rose and fired half-blinded. Thank God she was using a weak torch.

'Yes, I'm afraid I would shoot you lady, pregnant or no.' I told her corpse.

I knew the 'pregnant' claim was an add-on by a quick-thinking enemy, an appeal to my humanity in the hope of delaying me for another second. Instead, it had betrayed her deceit.

'Shoot them in the neck' Frank had told me 'That way when they're blown to pieces there will be little chance of bullet holes being found.'

I saw the sense in that, their limbs and heads would be torn off and mangled almost beyond recognition. However, even after suffering a huge blast, the torso tended to stay fairly intact. Bullet holes found post-mortem would make the bombers martyrs and we Brits murderers.

'And what if I can't manage that, Frank? It will be dark you know. That's bloody difficult shooting.'

Frank's icy blue eyes had glinted their displeasure, his face set hard. Gone the laid-back attitude 'If you *fail*' he emphasized the word to indicate I'd better not, 'just get the buggers dead, OK? We'll sort the flack out later.' It was clear Frank had not wanted his plan questioned.

'We picked you because you're supposed to be the best. Now fucking prove it,' his voice was harsh, his cut-glass accent radiating disdain.

Yes, there had been an edge to Frank's briefing. Now I knew why, and I was not happy.

Inspecting my handiwork, I saw both bodies had large gory exit wounds made by my 9 mm hollow-point bullets.

I picked up her flashlight and examined the bomber's equipment. Bloody hell, she'd meant business. There were three trembler switches, a mercury tilt switch, a pressure plate and several detonators as well as an American made timer.

Each device had its own power supply and would work independently but was also interconnected so that cutting a wire on one would collapse electromagnets, allowing contacts to close. Once armed, these devices needed only a slight nudge to detonate the explosives. After setting the timer and arming it there was no going back. Switching off the timer would also cause detonation.

I grudgingly admired the bomber's handiwork. By utilizing a clever prewired loom, a complex bomb could be set in minutes.

On top of the fertilizer was a kilo of the powerful commercial plastic explosive, Semtex1A. That was the booster charge. For some reason I couldn't explain even to myself, I cut the charge in half with my jackknife and wrapped one half in my handkerchief before pocketing it along with a detonator and the tilt switch.

I connected a detonator to the timer, switching it on. If there was a fault it would blow the detonator and not the main charge making it a nasty but survivable shock. I then pushed the detonator into the plastic.

Now I had to consider the timing. After pondering for a few seconds, I decided three minutes would have to do. I had to get clear, but if I left it too long the driver might return, discover the bodies and flee. There could be no witnesses.

I took a final look around. The street as far as I could see was empty, but there was no way I would risk leaving by the front door.

I lifted the top bag and placed the Semtex beneath it, then flicked the arming switch to set the timer going.

Making my way carefully down the alley at the rear of the shop I kept my pistol out and ready. It was highly unlikely any watcher would still be there, but caution was everything in this game.

I heard a movement to my front left, slight, yes, but a movement. I froze, watching, listening, breathing suspended, my eyes straining to penetrate the inky blackness. I was still too near the target, I had to move soon, or risk being killed by the blast. After thirty seconds the movement came again, I raised my weapon my finger on the hair-trigger. A cat yowled its protest at me for invading its territory, leapt off the waste bin and fled.

Breathing a sigh of relief, I moved on as quickly as caution permitted. I had no more time to waste.

Reaching the end of the alley I turned right along the gable end of the terrace of shops and stopped. Peering around the corner into the dimly lit street, I was about to cross, when the car suddenly returned, its headlights illuminated the gloom down to where I was hiding. It pulled up outside the target; I was a scant fifty metres away, too bloody close for comfort.

The car waited outside the shop, its engine idling. A long minute dragged by; I couldn't move. If the driver saw me, he might take off and then there'd be a witness.

Sweet and Sour

The man left the car, gun in hand, glancing nervously up and down the empty street.

I watched him through the gap between the drainpipe and the wall, he checked his watch, then went to the door and knocked. As if in answer the bomb detonated.

The blinding flash lit up the street as bright as the sun, the pressure wave crushing my eardrums. I flattened myself hard against the wall. I knew I was safe from the blast but not from falling debris. A huge brick landed not a foot in front of me, shattering into fragments. A small shard of glass slashed my ear causing me to gasp in shock, blood spilling down my neck and into my collar.

It was another forty seconds before bricks, slates and more shards stopped raining down. Sirens started their electronic hee-hawing in the distance. It was time to go.

*

In the debriefing, I contained my fury. There was no point in showing how pissed off I was, not yet anyway, not until I knew for certain. After going over the briefing yet again I realised that Frank had never once used the name Declan, substituting 'he' or 'him,' 'the bomber' or 'the targets.'

I slumped sullenly into an armchair as far away from the desk as I could get, staring defiantly, daring Frank to ask me to sit closer.

I was ignored as Frank continued to write in a document folder with studied indifference. Finally, he looked up.

'How did it go, Jack?' He smiled weakly, 'I heard you were injured, nothing serious I hope?'

I ignored his questions staring for a full ten seconds before answering, my emotions in turmoil. 'Deadly Declan turned out to be Deadly Delores' I said, carefully keeping my voice neutral. Frank's eyes flicked away for just a fraction of a second, but it was the final proof that the man had known. 'But of course, you knew that at the briefing' I added.

Frank started a denial, but I cut him off abruptly, 'don't bullshit me, Frank, OK?' I continued to stare unblinkingly. Christ, I wanted to punch the devious bastard.

'They thought you might not do the job if you knew' he said lamely 'Declan was killed in a drink driving incident a week ago, but the job had already been scheduled. He'd taught his girlfriend all he knew. She simply took his place, and the PIRA didn't announce the death to keep his legend alive.'

'So, that's why you didn't give the job to the Special Air Service, eh? Most of 'em are known to be squeamish about killing women, and you didn't want any prisoners.'

Frank's face reddened 'Sorry Jack, it wasn't my idea, it was them, it came from above.'

My temper snapped, 'just who the hell are 'them' Frank? When you recruited me for the hit team, I told you I would only work for you and not for any damned buck-passing committee.'

'Aw, c'mon Jack, everybody has a boss, you know that. I...'

I got up and crossed rapidly to Frank. The fist I wanted to slam into his face, I slammed onto the desk instead.

'Those Staff Officer types in Whitehall are too interested in their fucking careers to give a shit about us blokes in the field Frank, and you know it. You should have told me and bollocks to their orders.' Normally I control my feelings well, but this was a betrayal of trust. The job was dangerous enough without my own side playing me. I was furious that Frank was playing down the significance of it, siding with the interfering bastards.

'Again, all I can say is sorry, Jack. Now, can we press on please?' he said impatiently. He was trying to brush it all aside like my life didn't matter. Well, it mattered to me.

'No, we can't' I shouted 'sorry isn't good enough Frank. I will not be manipulated by a bunch of Whitehall wankers who know three-fifths of fuck-all about life in the field.'

I had to fight for control whilst I continued to stare at the bastard. He looked down at his hands, unable to meet my gaze.

It was a while before I could speak calmly again 'well, you can find yourself another man mate, I resign…. as of now.'

'Be reasonable, Jack, it was only a small omission.'

'Small omission my arse Frank, it was a breach of trust. Surprise damn near got me killed.'

'Believe me, Jack, it'll never happen again.'

'You've got that bit right, Frank' I said 'there's no such thing as ninety-nine per cent total trust. You've blown it.' I turned and walked swiftly to the door, the anger seething inside me.

'Where the hell do you think you're going Sergeant Major Belthorn? This meeting isn't over yet.'

I turned, 'yes it fuckin' well is' I bawled, 'and don't pull that rank shit on me Major whatever-the-fuck-your-real-name-is.' with that I marched out slamming the door.

In our unit, we never used rank for practical reasons. If we were working in the field together and under stress, we didn't want any slip-ups like calling someone sir. Frank had deliberately reintroduced rank, attempting to control me. He was on a loser there.

In my room, I pulled out a bottle of Bushmills and poured myself a stiff one, my thoughts dark.

Resigning from the two-man hit team was a big no-no and I knew it. Once in, there was no way out,

Sweet and Sour

until you either stopped a bullet or they released you at the end of your tour.

Our unit rarely killed anyone, only those otherwise untouchables who caused hugely disproportionate damage, the ones beyond the reach of the law. The other guy on the hit team was still a probationer, fully trained but lacking in field experience. Frank wouldn't give up.

14th Company (The Detachment) was an offshoot of the British Army Intelligence Corps that did the dirty, deniable stuff. Most other soldiers didn't even know we existed. Our main task was gathering intelligence to brief the Special Air Service on covert ops. We also spread half-truths, rumours and subtle lies to keep the enemy on the hop.

The IRA and the Provisional IRA (The Provos) were deeply suspicious of each other, and we exploited this schism to the full. If they were busy fighting amongst themselves, they would have less time to focus on murdering soldiers and policemen.

Declan Dooley had not only killed three ordnance experts but also many innocent civilians, too. Captured, he would have been a hero, a symbol of resistance inspiring others. Imprisoned, he would have been able to pass on his knowledge. Now, Dooley was just another failed bomber who'd made his last mistake taking two comrades with him. The legend was ended. Bleeding-heart Liberals would not be bleating about the so-called 'moral' issues, calling for a public enquiry. No propaganda victory for the Provos, no cloak of victimhood to be paraded in America to raise funds. OK, so it wasn't Declan Dooley I'd killed, but that hardly mattered now.

Frank would leave me alone tonight, of that, I was sure. He wouldn't report my insubordination until his routine visit to Army HQ two days hence. In the meantime, he'd try to win me round. They couldn't afford a loose cannon in their midst. If it ever got out what we were up to the repercussions would echo not only around the Government but the rest of the world, too. It would generate huge sympathy and funds for the enemy.

Receiving duff information at a briefing was a common enough occurrence. Intelligence is far from an exact science, and I accepted that, but deliberately omitting vital information went beyond the pale. If I allowed them to get away with it this time, they'd do it again when they deemed it expedient.

Fuck 'em all, I thought. I threw back my drink and poured another one. 'Fuck 'em all to hell' I muttered then I got slowly and grandly shit-faced.

Frank called me to his office the next day, 'have you thought any more about what you threatened last night?'

'Yes,' I said, 'and my decision stands.'

He let out a long sigh, 'look, man, they aren't going to let you resign, you must know that, surely?'

Sweet and Sour

We bandied the issue about for a few minutes before he said 'I'm sorry Jack, but I'll have to report this. I'll leave it to the last minute until I go to HQ tomorrow, but then my hands will be tied.'

'OK,' I said, 'I'll think on it' knowing full well I wouldn't. My mind was made up. Sure, they'd find a way to take me out and they had a lot more resources than me, however, I had half a plan.

The next day I was waiting by the gate as Frank drove up. He stopped and lowered the window of the Jag 'You got something to tell me, Jack?'

'Yeah,' I said, 'will you drop me at the shops? I need some stuff.'

He looked surprised, 'Get in.'

We drove half a mile to the shops in silence, he was expecting me to tell him I'd changed my mind and was back on the team. I knew that wasn't an option now that I'd shown prolonged defiance of authority. They couldn't live with that; these Whitehall warrior types who thought they were so fucking superior. At best I'd be given the most dangerous of jobs until, inevitably, I got unlucky. At worst, they'd engineer my demise.

'Thanks' I told Frank as I opened the car door 'you go ahead and make that report.'

'Jack, are you serious? Don't do this.'

'Bye Frank' I said as I closed the door and made my way into the shop.

He drove off. I watched from the shop, seeing him stop at the traffic lights a hundred yards away. When the lights changed, he turned left up the steep hill towards HQ.

I heard the explosion as the tilt switch and Semtex did their job. HQ would never get his report now, and I'd survive. Maybe my next boss wouldn't be such an arsehole.

As I said, I am not a nice man.

Note: This story is the first chapter of my full-length novel The Negotiator available as a download or a paperback on Amazon books.

Weasel Words

Sometimes drastic situations require thinking outside the box to provide novel solutions.

'Honestly Granddad I'm at my wit's end, they were at it again last night until four this morning. I don't know how much longer I can go on.' Jenny sniffed and wiped a tear from her eye. 'They have rap music blaring night and day, and their language is disgusting. Little Billy is terrified of playing in the garden, yesterday they threw a big slab of concrete over the fence, it could have killed him if it had hit him.'

The final straw had been when Jenny came home from her part-time job that afternoon to find that an obscenity had been scrawled across her window in human excrement.

Mick looked serious; his normally smooth brow was knit in a deep frown he hated to see his granddaughter like this. It was the third time this month she'd come over to ask if she and Billy his three-year-old grandson could stay the night. Her nieghbours, a family called Witzell, known locally as the Weasels, were one of the county's worst antisocial problem families. They seemed to revel in antagonizing their nieghbours, appearing in court and being reported in the local press seemed to amuse them.

The 'Weasel' family consisted of Alice Witzell the matriarch, her husband Jock a giant of a man who came and went as he pleased between his home and that of his pregnant lover, two sons Keylon and Jago aged sixteen and eighteen respectively and their fourteen-year-old sister Jaynie-Shannon.

Keylon and Jago rode around the district on a noisy motorcycle or sat on it in the garden revving the engine for what seemed like hours at a time. They partied most nights getting drunk and fighting and on more than one occasion they had urinated through Jenny's letterbox. Jaynie-Shannon delighted in screeching obscenities at Jenny every time she saw her in her garden.

True, the local authorities had threatened to evict them but that was a long process. The threat of eviction served only to goad the Witzells on to even more outrageous behaviour. Lately, they had bought a large fierce-looking dog which, with some predictability, they had named Tyson. The animal spent its time chained in the garden barking when the lads were not parading it around the streets showing it off and intimidating folk. It seemed no one had enough courage to stand up to this family from hell.

If Jenny protested to the Witzells they only sneered at her, if she called the police, they threatened

Sweet and Sour

her and her son. As a single mother, she felt isolated and trapped with no one to turn to. The police had other priorities and were too slow to respond effectively, the other so-called 'Authorities' had had a word with the Witzells on numerous occasions; the Social Services personnel were mostly too scared to call. When the local council people did eventually call to 'gather evidence' as they put it, they came at nine-thirty in the morning when all was quiet because the Witzell's were still in bed nursing hangovers.

Jenny's shoulders sagged, her face pinched and miserable. 'When I complain to the council, granddad, all I get is the runaround "We're doing our best Ms. Hartnell, it's difficult to find appropriate accommodation for these families Ms. Hartnell, blah, blah bloody blah Ms. Hartnell..."

Jenny went upstairs and prepared the spare room for her and Billy. Why she told granddad Mick her woes she didn't know, he was an old man for heaven's sake. What could he do about it, a gentle old soul like him? If she told her parents they would simply recommend that she forgive them and pray to the Lord for a solution. She'd prayed fervently but the Lord seemed as reluctant to intervene as the local authorities were.

Granddad Mick, a sixty-eight-ear-old pensioner, was a widower and a good listener whom she adored. It was he, poor fellow, who was her shoulder to cry on. As she made up the beds, Jenny little suspected that mild-mannered Mick was about to become involved with the Witzells.

*

Mick was as fit and active as a man of his age could be. He went swimming three or four times a week and walked everywhere weather permitting. He also had a keen intelligence coupled with a readiness to act when needed. He was an ex-Royal Marine Commando, though he spoke little of his service. He now sat deep in thought.

Jenny finished preparing the room and went downstairs. 'I'm going to pick Billy up from the nursery school now gramps can I make you a brew before I go?'

'No love, I'm fine, you get on.'

As soon as she had left the house Mick went out to his garden shed 'Hmmnn now let me see' he mused to himself. Oh, yes, he thought, I'll need to buy some of that and one of those. After rummaging around for ten minutes he'd assembled an assortment of odd articles. There was a small wooden stake, a funnel, some fishing line and a roll of gaffer tape which he stuffed into an old haversack, he then locked the shed, checked his watch and saw he still had time to do a little research online before his granddaughter returned.

That evening, with Billy bathed and put to bed, Mick poured them both a drink and they settled into

Sweet and Sour

comfortable armchairs but instead of putting the television on Mick said he had something to tell her.

'Jenny, I think I may have a solution to your problem. It's one I cannot divulge just now 'cos I'm still finalising the details.'

Jenny looked dubious 'What on earth are you talking about gramps? You can't possibly take on the Witzells at your age.'

'Who said I was going to?' he queried, a sly twinkle in his eye. 'All I'm going to do is write them a note, a few words of advice you might say.'

Jenny's jaw dropped, she stared at him as though he'd taken leave of his senses. 'A note?' She asked incredulously 'what the hell good do you think note will do Gramps?'

'Ah well,' Mick said conspiratorially 'This will be a special note, one that commands attention and will be taken seriously and that's all I'm saying on the subject.'

Jenny jerked upright, 'like hell, Gramps' she almost shouted, 'I want you to promise me you'll not do anything hare-brained or put yourself in danger.' She looked at him through narrowed eyes, she knew, gentle creature that he was, he could be as stubborn as a mule and impossible to move once his mind was made up. 'Just promise me you'll not approach them will you gramps? I couldn't bear it if anything bad were to happen to you.'

'I promise darling girl, now I'm off to bed for an early night, I have a busy day tomorrow.'

*

Four days later, preparations complete, Mick got into his car with the small rucksack and drove three miles to park a mile from his destination. He left the car in a quiet residential cul-de-sac, donned a wide-brimmed hat to shield his face from street cameras, and walked to his granddaughter's house. He didn't stop but walked slowly past on the opposite side of the street glancing at the Witzell's house, taking in the details he would need. From the back of the house, he could hear Tyson barking at nothing in particular. On the litter-strewn patch of earth that passed for a front garden, Keylon and Jago were kicking a football about whilst through the open front door came the blare of gangsta rap.

At five-thirty the following morning Mick crept down the side of Jenny's house in the first glimmer of dawn and into her back garden. Over the broken fence Tyson started barking as Mick threw the dog a piece of meat he had prepared for the occasion. It was nothing lethal, just enough to put the dog to sleep for a few hours.

Mick waited until the animal had succumbed to the sedative then crept silently to the Witzell's front door where he lifted the flap on the letterbox and made his delivery. After that swift action, he pushed an envelope half though with a surgically gloved hand

Sweet and Sour

then moved into the front garden where he crouched down some four yards from the house and busied himself. Less than two minutes later he was making his way home job done.

At seven-thirty a.m. Alice Witzell awoke with the feeling that something was wrong, she didn't know what it was, but something had disturbed her slumber at what was, for her, an ungodly hour. She scratched her tousled head for a minute slowly gaining a higher level of consciousness; something was definitely wrong.

Climbing out of bed she donned a grubby housecoat and a pair of slippers and went to the bedroom door. It was upon opening the door that the smell hit her. It was at once familiar, but she couldn't quite put a name to it. The rest of the house was quiet save for the snoring coming from the boys' bedroom. She checked her daughter's bedroom; the girl was sound asleep.

Feeling uneasy, she made her way slowly downstairs, her unease growing with every step she took. The smell was getting stronger and stronger. At the bottom, she saw the white envelope sticking through the letterbox. As she went to retrieve it, she, at last, recognised the smell, it was paraffin. As it soaked into her slippers wetting her feet Alice let out a strangled squawk, leaping out of the slippers and running into the living room. Once in there she tore open the envelope and took out the single sheet of neatly typed paper. Her finger followed the words and her lips moved as she slowly read:

Dear problem family,

We who live around here will tolerate no more of your vile behaviour. The paraffin. was not lit on this occasion as it was meant to give you fair warning. You will behave in a civilised manner, get rid of the dog and show consideration for your nieghbours or move out. Your choice.

Alice's hands shook as she realised the full implication of the threat. She dropped the letter and ran upstairs screaming for the children to wake up. Dashing into her daughter's room she shook her awake then ran into the boys' room still screaming hysterically. The lads were not best pleased with being disturbed and started cursing her.

When they had calmed their mother down enough to discover what had happened, Jago, with the stupidity and bravado of immature youth, threw on his jeans and ran downstairs shouting about showing these bastards who is boss around here. As he tore open the front door the fishing line Mick had attached to the door knocker pulled tautly and detonated the large industrial firework he had tied to a stake in the garden. There was a bright flash and an almighty bang that blew out two windows of the Witzell's house.

The ashen-faced youth leapt back into the house and dived behind the sofa screaming for his mother. Meanwhile, the terrified Jaynie-Shannon cowered under her bed trembling and whimpering, losing control of her bladder. Keylon had run out of the back door to fetch Tyson for reasons he alone knew only to find the animal was sleeping peacefully and could not be aroused.

The long-suffering nieghbours, Jenny included, thinking the bang was just another episode of anti-social behaviour on the part of the weasels didn't even bother calling the police but, after looking through their curtains for a moment, went back to their slumbers, after all, it was Sunday morning.

Later that morning Jenny came to Mick's house 'Granddad, you'll never guess what's happened?' Jenny was practically dancing with delight 'Mrs Witzell said good morning to me and actually smiled. A little while later she came to the door and said they were moving out today and staying with relatives 'til they found somewhere else, and would I keep an eye on their house until they could arrange for their stuff to be moved.'

'Oh, that *is* good news, Jenny' said Mick, smiling broadly, 'I wonder what caused that?'

'It must be the power of prayer, granddad like mum and dad said.' She laughed, 'the thought of you writing them a letter Gramps. Really!' She kissed his forehead, her eyes moist with love 'It was so sweet of you, my darling Gramps, but it couldn't possibly have worked.'

Mick smiled beatifically, 'No, my dear, I suppose you're right.'

Sweet and Sour

The Seer

Nine-year-old Temujin controlled his galloping horse with his knees, bow at the ready. The rabbit was turning and twisting in its effort to escape. As a child of the plains and the son of a chief this was second nature to him. He shot, letting out a cry of exultation when his arrow struck home. His friend Jamulka, close behind him, let out a whoop of joy. They would eat well today.

That night by the campfire replete with roasted rabbit Temujin said 'Jamulka read the fire.'

'My father is the Shaman Temujin, not me.'

'But you have his gift, the whole tribe know that. Why did my father order us to hunt alone?'

'Because of the meeting with the Tartars, he doesn't trust them. You need no special powers to know that Temujin.'

Temujin's hot temper flared 'I am the chief's son Jamulka. You will read.'

Jamulka glared 'take your hand from your knife, Temujin, I will not read under threat.'

Temujin glared but complied. 'Read.'

Jamulka took some poppy powder from his pouch and took a twig, scraping glowing embers into his bowl. He sprinkled the powder, muttering an incantation. After inhaling the smoke deeply, he stared into the fire.

'What do you see Jamulka. Am I to become a great chief?' Temujin's impatience annoyed the other boy, but he held his peace.

'Better you remain ignorant my friend.'

Temujin seized Jamulka's shoulder violently 'tell me or by the gods....'

'What? You'll murder me? As you will your half-brother?'

'Why will I do that?'

'Because he bars your way to power.'

Temujin glowered 'If your prophecy proves false, I'll have your tongue cut out so read truthfully.'

Jamulka stared back defiantly 'We are supposed to be friends, Temujin, our fathers are friends, mine ranks only second to yours yet you speak to me like a slave. I will not read for you until you apologise.'

Temujin stared hard at Jamulka and saw that he was serious. No other boy in the tribe would dare to defy him. He took a deep breath; apology did not come easily to him. Sensing that he might need Jamulka now and in the future, he smiled. 'You are brave to defy me Jamulka and your courage deserves reward therefore I apologise.'

'Very well then, you shall know.' Jamulka inhaled more poppy smoke and stared again into the coals for what seemed an age, his dark brown eyes growing wide. A tear ran down his cheek as he addressed his friend. 'We must return to the tribe at dawn,' he said, his voice trembling.

'My father ordered us away for a week, to defy him would be to earn us a beating.'

'Your father is already dead, Temujin, murdered by the Tartars.'

'You lie' Temujin shrieked, leaping to his feet and drawing his knife.

Jamulka remained seated, his face sad. He spoke calmly, 'what your father feared has happened. He sent us hunting without finery or escort so that we attracted no attention. For who would take notice of two village boys out hunting rabbits? He wiped his tears on the back of his hand, ignoring the drawn knife. 'Your father was very wise.'

Temujin, faced with Jamulka's sad face and calm manner sat back down, dropping his knife. He looked bewildered and far too old for his years in the flickering firelight.

'Tell me, Jamulka, he said after a long pause 'how am I to be the leader of my tribe as a mere boy?'

'Your time is not yet Temujin. The tribe will reject you. You will become a slave. You will escape, but only after learning patience and an understanding of people. You will unite all the tribes, building a great new empire and be called Khan. Millions will perish cursing your name. You will die young.'

'There, now you know, and I am bound to you forever.'

Temujin threw his arms around his friend and wept for the last time in his life 'May the heavens have mercy on us both.'

Stirling Karma

The bench bore a small brass plaque inscribed "Peter 02 01 1999- 04 03 2021" It was sited beneath a shady oak tree overlooking the broad valley. John sat, pain pulsing in his heart, tears partially clouding his vision. He was staring unseeing at the beauty that lay before him, remembering. He came here every Friday hail, rain or shine and had done since the funeral to sit and mourn Today, though, would be different.

After half an hour, John wiped his eyes on his sleeve. He rose to leave when a movement on the path below caught his attention. The rough-looking young man was carrying a hold-all, hurrying and looking around him furtively. He looked everywhere except up. John was curious, he rarely saw anyone in this remote place. Hiker's carried haversacks, not hold-all's and this chap was not dressed for a country walk. He stopped, looking almost straight at John without seeing him. John realised that dressed in dark clothes he would be invisible against the tree trunk under the oak's deep shade. The guy placed the hold-all behind a lone ash tree then took out his phone and sent a text before hurrying on.

Old habits die hard. John made his way down the hill instinctively using every available bush and fold in the landscape as cover from the track. He found the bag, it was heavy. The zip was locked, no problem. He took his ballpoint pen and pushed it through the zip spreading it wide. It would rezip and nobody would know.

The familiar item on top shocked him. He took it, resealing and replacing the bag. He knew the purpose of the bag and knew someone would be collecting it soon. John concealed himself behind a bush a few yards away from the ash tree and waited. He didn't have to wait long.

The ugly man in the tracksuit jogged up, squinted around him, then went straight for the hold-all. He hefted it, looked puzzled, then drew a key and opened the bag.

'Looking for this.'

The man jumped up, his mouth and eyes opening wide. His hand flew to his waistband.

'Don't.'

The guy stopped, assessing the situation, regaining his composure. 'Careful with that thing granddad, do you even know what it is?' he sneered.

'It's a Stirling sub-machine gun, 9 mm, fires around 350 rounds a minute.' His face was calm, almost serene. 'I checked the magazine, there are thirty rounds all pointing at your guts.'

Sweet and Sour

The man stroked his chin apprehensively 'Listen, pop, you don't know just who the hell I am, so I'll give you a chance, yeah?' He took a step forward put the gun down and walk away and I'll forget I ever saw you, OK?'

John unclipped the folding butt and put the weapon to his shoulder aiming at the man's leg. 'One more step and you'll be limping for life.'

The man stopped, hands spread his sneer less certain 'Maybe we can do a deal, pop. Yeah?'

'Take your pistol out slowly and kick it over here.'

'Fuck off, you won't shoot.'

John thumbed the safety catch forward once to the single-shot position then lowered his aim sending a bullet between the man's feet.

The startled man jumped back spreading his arms 'OK, OK Pop, don't lose it, OK?' He reached slowly under his coat and withdrew a Glock 17 with forefinger and thumb. He dropped it but didn't kick it over, a move not lost on John.

'Drug money, ain't it?'

'That's got fuck-all to do with you old man, you don't know what you're getting yourself into. Piss off while you still have the chance.'

John remained impassive. 'What's your name, big shot?'

'I'm Jack McCready, everyone's heard of me, Benton Street Crew.' He looked at his watch 'there's two men back at the pub, they'll come hunting if I'm not back in five minutes then god help you.'

John adjusted his aim and fired a single shot, smashing McCready's knee. Shock and horror filled McCready's face as he fell screaming to the floor clutching his shattered knee. John watched him writhing, his face blank, his eyes cold. He waited until McCready's screams subsided into moans as his victim rocked left and right clutching his blood-soaked jeans.

John went forward, pocketing the Glock. 'You are going to tell me about this money and the gun mate, or I'll shoot a few more of your joints away.' He aimed at McCready's ankle.

'Ok, mate, Ok, it's drugs money, OK? The gun is part payment. We don't trust the guys who we supply; they don't trust us. We drop off the drugs at one location and simultaneously they drop off the money at another, always different places, all done by WhatsApp.'

'And your friends will be here soon, or was that a bluff?'

'No bluff mate, you're one dead arsehole.'

John took the hold-all and moved to his right up the hill out of sight of McCready then he circled back to cross the track. He found the remnants of a dry-stone wall and waited.

Sweet and Sour

Two men, machine pistols in hand, came running down the track. McCready pointed up the hill, 'up there, old guy, the bastard took the money.

'Hey, arseholes.'

They whipped around, one firing a burst into the ground in his panic. John put a short burst through each chest. He walked back to McCready noting the terror in his eyes. he asked 'who the fuck are you man? Who sent you?'

'John Portland, ex-Royal Marines weapons instructor, karma sent me. You lot picked the wrong guy.'

McCready looked into John's cold blue eyes and saw no mercy there. 'For fuck's sake, please, why don't you just take the money and piss off? No one will come after you, I swear.'

'Yeah, right.' John aimed McCready's guts, and the drug dealer's voice rose to a screech. 'For Christ's sake mate, please, don't kill me, I got kids.'

'So have I, and grandkids, too. Thanks to scum like you, I've now got one less. Twenty-two he was, knifed over a lousy fifty quid drug debt.' John switched to automatic and emptied the magazine into McCready's stomach.

Wiping the weapons clean, he dropped them on the path then made his way back up to the bench. His body was shaking but his mind was calm. 'Well, Pctcr, that won't bring you back, son, but maybe it will spare a few others.'

The charity Reclaimed from Addiction UK had a parcel delivered to their office by a courier in a full-face motorcycle helmet and gloves. It contained ninety-five thousand pounds. There was no note, no explanation. A stolen motorcycle was recovered nearby.

Part Two

Piles of Trouble

At a barbeque last summer, Bill, my thick-as-a-brick next-door neighbour was boring me mindless with his medical problems. We were both a bit worse for the drink, he much more so than me.

'My haemorrhoids itch like crazy' he told me. 'They drive me mad at times.'

He began clawing vigorously at himself, quite putting me off my burger. 'Ah' I quipped, laying aside my now unwanted food, 'I have a great remedy for that, works every time.'

Of course, Bill wanted to know so I told him 'Take two scotch bonnet chilies and crush them to a paste, stir in two tablespoonsful of tabasco sauce and a tablespoon of salt. Apply this paste liberally to the affected area, you won't feel an itch for a long while after that.'

My little joke fell flat so I wandered off to find more congenial company.

Half an hour after the barbeque had ended, I heard hideous, agonised shrieks coming from Bill's back garden. I looked out to see him running around in circles and jumping up and down. He was dressed only in his T-shirt. His fat bottom was naked, and his

Sweet and Sour

wedding tackle was flapping like a fish on a riverbank. Both his hands were clutching wildly at his buttocks as he ran blindly into a patch of stinging nettles that grew from his compost heap, falling headlong into it. His short fat legs thrashed the air as his screeching grew even louder.

I couldn't see clearly after that for the laughter tears streaming from my eyes. Bill then leapt up, still screaming like the damned, and dived, buttocks first, into his birdbath. There he sat scouring water into his builder's cleavage like a man possessed whilst howling for help. This frantic action caused him to accidentally push some of the chilli paste inside himself and his screams went up an octave.

I staggered out to help him, my drunken head bemused as to what I could do to relieve his plight.

'Oh, Jaysus, it's inside me' he screamed. The birdbath collapsed, dumping his on the lawn where he lay convulsing and screaming 'fer Christ's sake, somebody shoot me.'

An idea dawned, I grabbed his garden hose, and, turning it on, I rolled him over. His head and knees were now on the grass, his backside sticking high in the air.

I inserted the hosepipe to flush him out and another scream came from behind me. I turned to see my wife Mabel staring aghast, her hands clasped to the sides of her head, her mouth agape in horror. She had come out to see what all the noise was about only to find me working a garden hose up Bill's jacksie and him shouting 'Oh, yes! Don't stop, please don't stop.'

Poor Mabel let out a long despairing wail and fainted, flopping face first into our fishpond. I left Bill to go and rescue Mabel but tripped over the damned hose and sprawled on top of her, cracking my head on an ornamental stone frog.

We were rescued by two police officers who appeared around the side of the house to investigate reports of a murder taking place that another neighbour had reported. They found me and Mabel unconscious, face down in the pond and Bill ramming the hose up his bottom crying 'yes, oh yes' with great passion.

It took some explaining I can tell you. The coppers took fifty minutes and a full box of Mabel's tissues to complete their statement.

Bill's haemorrhoids haven't itched once since that day but he's still not talking to me, the ungrateful bugger.

Greasy Grice

It was a combination of charm and low cunning that marked Bombardier Bob (Greasy) Grice out from the crowd. He had been a sergeant (twice) then got himself busted down to the basic rank of gunner. His great character, initiative and quick wits had got him promoted again. Bob had his fans among the officers, but Sergeant Majors were harder to fool. One had described him as: "slicker than a blob of snot on a glass handrail" and he wasn't joking.

Posted to Germany in 1967, Bob was watching his P's and Q's. With one year left to serve, regaining his third stripe would increase his pension considerably.

The Regiment was in the middle of Luneburg Heide on a long exercise when an opportunity in the form of his Battery Commander's personal problem presented itself.

'Ah, Bombardier Grice, just the man.'

Bob jumped to attention as, Major John Thetford-Beavis, addressed him.

Bob beamed a smile, his craggy face resembling a busted boot. 'How can I help you, sir?'

'It's the Battery cook, Bombardier, he's burned his hand rather badly, I'm afraid.'

Bob let his face sag to bloodhound sadness 'Oh dear, sir, that's most unfortunate.'

'Yes, bombardier, and we have the brigadier and the colonel dining in the mess this evening. I'm told you're rather a dab hand with field rations so I'm appointing you chef.'

Most junior NCO's would have despaired to hear this. Not Bob, he saw only opportunity. 'Thank you, sir, it will be an honour, though I'd like to suggest, if I may, sir?'

'What's that, Bombardier?'

'For a hundred Deutsche marks or so, I could nip down to the nearest village and obtain some proper supplies, sir.' He paused whilst this idea sank into the officer's consciousness. 'After all sir, we don't get many opportunities to impress the brigadier, sir.'

The major rubbed his chin for a moment and decided that making a favourable impression on the Brigadier could do his career no harm at all. 'You know bombardier, you're absolutely right, and I suppose mess funds can stand it.' The money was promptly found and handed over.

Bob grabbed four of his most trusted gunners and drove the Major's Land Rover down the lane. His initial idea had been to drive to the nearest Gasthof for a quick drink then go and see what kind of deal he could do in the village leaving himself a decent commission.

Sweet and Sour

After a mile, the sharply bending lane forced the Landrover to slow right down. It was then that Bob saw a golden opportunity. He stopped near a farm gate and sized up the situation in a flash. A tractor was working far away on the horizon. Yes, he thought, distinct possibilities, certainly worth a try.

'Right, two of you, out and pick me those blackberries. You others into that orchard and grab some cooking apples. Look sharp now.'

Bob walked up to the farm, circling around the side to where he'd seen a hen pen. He knew a bit about chickens having been once fostered on a farm. There, strutting about in all his glory, was the most beautiful golden rooster he'd ever seen.

Making sure he wasn't observed, Bob climbed into the pen and grabbed the prize bird. Tucking it under his arm then he marched up to the farmhouse and knocked on the door.

'Ja mein Herr?' queried the farmer's wife.

'Sprechen sie English bitter?' Bob asked in his broad Yorkshire accent.

The farmer's wife was a rotund lady in her mid-forties with a florid face that matched the red apron she was wearing. 'Nein. Ein moment bitte.' She called over her shoulder 'Helga.'

A young girl of about fifteen appeared and her mother spoke rapidly to her.

Helga turned to Bob and said, 'my mother wants to know how she can help you und vie you are holding my father's cock?'

With a great effort, Bob kept his face straight, 'I'm returning it to you. It was in the lane; I almost ran over it. My Landrover went into the ditch but not to worry the damage is slight and my head will get better soon. He rubbed the side of his head with a rueful smile. He handed the bird to the girl with exaggerated care. 'I can see it's a valuable bird. I'm so glad I managed to miss it.'

'Are you alright?' Helga's eyes were saucers of concern.

'Sure, I'm OK, just a bit shaken up,' he said in a tone that implied the opposite, 'I'm just glad your bird is OK.'

Helga translated for her mother who looked from the bird to Bob, her mouth agape, 'mein liebe Gott!' she exclaimed 'Kommen sie bitte hierein.'

'She wants you to come in' said Helga waving him into the large kitchen. Five minutes later, the cockrel having been restored to his adoring hens, Bob was ensconced in front of a blazing fire with a cold beer in his fist. He was telling Helga a tale of how he'd been ordered to provide a dinner for his officers, and he'd had to scrape together a few marks to buy food for them. Would they, by any chance, be able to sell him some as the village was a long way off and he didn't speak German.

Bob produced a pathetic looking handful of loose Deutsche marks and pfennigs from his pocket and proffered them, his face a picture of hopeful innocence.

Margot, the farmer's wife, asked through her daughter how many officers had he to feed.

'Oh, only ten or so' he said, cheerfully doubling the number.

Margot scurried away and produced a huge pile of wild boar cutlets plus heaps of fresh vegetables, some flour, sugar, milk, butter and eggs which she placed in a large cardboard box.

Waving away Bob's offer of payment she explained that the cockerel was her husband's pride and joy, saving its life would leave them forever in his debt.

Bob's eyes reflected deep gratitude that he almost felt. Smiling as benignly as a bishop bestowing a benediction, he bowed his way out of the kitchen with many danke schoen's, which he pronounced "donkey shin."

His lads were sitting around smoking and looking bored when Bob got back. They had completed their task of foraging some time ago. 'Where the hell have you been, Bom?' they asked in chorus.

'Buying food of course' said Bob, sounding aggrieved. 'Bloody hell lads, these farmers drive a hard bargain, tight sods the lot of 'em. Ninety-eight marks the buggers charged me for this lot.'

Shaking his head ruefully, he loaded his ill-gotten gains into the vehicle. Then he brightened, 'still, it's all fresh and there's enough for all of us. It saves us a long trip, too.'

The lads, of course, moaned because they'd expected a trip to the village and the chance of a few beers. Bob, on the other hand, needed them bright-eyed and alert to serve the meal that night.

Back at the camp, Bob worked hard and produced a delicious meal for the officers, rounded off by a superb apple and blackberry crumble with lashings of homemade custard.

Afterwards, he detailed his lads to do the washing up whilst he went to the mess tent to receive the congratulations due to a chef of his calibre.

Upon leaving, the Brigadier called Bob aside, 'That was a splendid meal bombardier, I'm most impressed that you produced it on a field kitchen. I think it's time we promoted you again. Do you think you can refrain from thumping people this time?'

Bob assured him that he was a reformed character and the senior officer departed.

Thereafter, Bob hung close around the back of the mess tent eavesdropping. He knew the officer clan very well and he had a sneaking suspicion of what was coming next. Well, not if he could help it.

Sure enough, his suspicions were confirmed when he heard his Battery Commander say, 'You know old Grice really surprised me tonight, I think I'll appoint

Sweet and Sour

him our cook for the rest of the exercise.' This was greeted by a wave of ascent from the other officers.

Bob smiled wryly and slipped away.

'Jones,' he called to the nearest gunner, 'go to the gun limber and fetch me some Swarfega and a nail brush.'

Jones jaw dropped, 'a nail brush, Bom? Where the 'ell am I supposed to get one of those? 'Arrod's?'

Bob scratched his ear, 'where's the Battery Sergeant Major?'

'He's gone on a reconnaissance, Bom,' said Jones.

Bob knew that 'reconnaissance' meant he'd buggered off for a few beers and wouldn't be back for ages.

'Righto, go to his tent and rescue his toothbrush, OK?'

'Yes Bom' said Jones and hurried away.

Bob scrubbed his hands until they were immaculate, his nails gleamed and the usual graphite grease that got ground into the creases of his skin was no longer in evidence. The BSM's toothbrush was duly returned, and bob awaited the summons to his Commanding Officer's presence.

'That was a superb meal bombardier, the Brigadier was delighted.'

'Oh, great, sir, I'm so glad you all enjoyed it, sir.' Bob's obsequious smile almost joined his ears.

'We enjoyed it so much that we are going to allow you to carry on cooking, Bombardier' he said condescendingly. 'I don't think we'll bother the Catering Corps for a replacement cook.'

'Oh, that is wonderful news, sir' Bob enthused, his face glowing with pride. 'Do you know sir, mixing that crumble was absolutely fantastic. I mean just look at my hands, sir. That flour and butter really gets all the grime from under my fingernails, sir, and all the gun grease is gone too, sir. It's magic.'

The Major's smile froze on his face as his gaze shifted from Bob's beaming countenance to his immaculate hands. 'Er, er... yes, yes, I see… Well, er, we'll talk about it again in the morning, Bombardier.'

The next day it was decided that, after further consideration, the officers had deemed it unfair to put upon Bob and that he should be allowed to continue his excellent work on the guns.

Bob professed his disappointment as inwardly his nefarious heart rejoiced. The Battery's biggest bullshitter had pulled it off again.

Respectable People.

Councilor Septimius Snodgrass, Lord Mayor of Brazdon, and staunch churchwarden surveyed his Sunday lunch table with a self-satisfied sigh. His children had done well for themselves as he, too, had done.

'How's the world of the PR executive coming along Amanda?' he asked his pretty daughter, 'still making a fortune, are we?'

Amanda smiled demurely 'hardly a fortune, dad, but I'm getting by.'

'What? A twenty-five-year-old with her own business, flat and a new car? I'd say you were doing handsomely.'

Amanda preened.

'Material things aren't everything, father.'

Septimius eyed his son, a curate, newly engaged to Sarah, a Bishop's daughter. 'You seem to be prospering in your own way, Angus. Soon have your own parish, I hear.'

Angus blushed, Sarah coughed, embarrassed, realising she should not have divulged that information without telling her fiancé. 'Nothing's settled yet, father.'

'That's quite enough Septimius' admonished Jane, his JP wife, 'you shouldn't embarrass him like that.'

Septimius sighed inwardly and took another slice of roast beef, his smile fixed. 'Yes, you're quite right, my dear, my apologies.'

Jane, or the plump frump as Septimus thought of her these days, had refused him yet again last night. At fifty-five he was still extremely active. He remembered telling a colleague at a boozy formal dinner that he was once a night and Jane was once a fortnight. They'd laughed and changed the subject, but it irked him. Once a fortnight, he thought, if only!

He needed to do something, but an affair was out of the question. They were pillars of the community, affairs always got found out, shame and disgrace followed.

*

The following Friday Septimius took Jane to an upmarket restaurant. He plied her with a large gin and tonic aperitif followed by a bottle of her favourite Chablis Premier Cru with dinner. Septimus made a real effort at romantic conversation. He reached for her hand 'remember our honeymoon darling? How we made love all night?'

'A rainy week in Blackpool in that awful boarding house with terrible food. How can I ever forget?'

His smile was a little pained 'I was referring to our lovemaking, dearest.'

Sweet and Sour

She smiled wistfully 'Yes, I suppose it was OK, and we were young, Septimus, that was almost thirty years ago.' She pulled her hand free, looking down at the sweet menu. 'I really shouldn't, but the sticky toffee pudding is my favourite.' She burped quietly and discreetly eased her belt.

Back home Septimus made a clumsy play for her.

'Oh, not tonight Septimius, I'm so full I'd burst.'

'Oh, for god's sake, Jane!' his face reddened as frustration washed through him, 'This is getting beyond a joke.'

'It's the change, dear,' she whined, 'can't you just watch porn or something?' It was the last straw.

*

Pinkie's Massage Emporium the advert read; full satisfaction guaranteed. Discreet entrance at the rear. It was in Sheffield, fifty miles away. That should be far enough he thought.

He parked half a mile away in a supermarket car park and, consulting his phone's satnav, walking the rest of the way. After a careful look around, he slid inside. He was greeted by a frowsy middle-aged bottle blonde who took his money and showed him into a dimly lit room.

'Take a shower, love, then relax, Mitzie will be with you shortly.'

Septimius's tummy fluttered. The power shower, fluffy towels, and the subtly scented air conspired to stimulate him. He lay naked face down on the bed growing erect with anticipation. He heard the door open behind him and soft footsteps crossing the floor. He felt her fingers lightly brush his buttocks and he shuddered, turning over.

They both screamed in horror.

'Amanda!'

'Dad!'

Short Backsides

'Oh, God, Jill, look who's crossing the road.'
Jill followed June's pointing finger.

'Oh, no, not Short Backsides, it can't be time for him already, surely?'

June looked at her sister, her mouth downturned, her pale blue eyes pained 'I'm afraid so, it has been six weeks at least.'

Jill groaned, she'd had a bad day so far, Billy, her five-year-old, had not wanted to go to school that morning and had to be dragged kicking and screaming. Isobel, his nine-month-old sister had puked on her on as she was being readied for nursery putting her way behind time.

The two women barbers braced themselves for what they knew would be a relentless onslaught of risqué old jokes and smutty remarks spouting from him and strained bonhomie on their part.

'Afternoon my bonny birds' cried Warren R Sowell, aka Short Backsides, grinning broadly as he breezed into the shop. He glanced around the empty waiting area 'no hot lovers in pursuit of you both today I see, well, great. No one to share you with my wicked, winsome wenches.'

'Afternoon Warren' said Jill, forcing a smile 'I'll be with you in a minute. She stepped out into the backyard of the shop she and June had inherited from their late father and lit a cigarette. She'd promised herself she would cut down on smoking and she had done, too, but old Short Backsides always brought out the need in her. He was a seventy-five-year-old potbellied little nerd, yet the silly old fool still thought he had sex appeal. And why did he insist on her cutting his hair, what was wrong with June doing it now and then?

She cringed inwardly drawing deeply on her cigarette at the thought of suffering the lewd remarks of this preening old goat. After a few more drags, she crushed the cigarette underfoot. Ah, well, best get on with it she thought, the sooner it's done the sooner he'll be gone.

She re-entered the shop to find him already sitting in her chair regaling June with some oft-repeated sleazy tale from his youth in Malaya and Borneo. 'That's what those Kuching bar girls were like in those days' she heard him say. Then he looked up 'oh there you are, at last, Jill. A quick shag, sorry, fag, was it?' he grinned inanely at his own crude joke.

Jill forced a smile, she would love to smack his silly face, to tell him to bugger off and not come back, but with Covid lockdown they needed every customer they could get. 'What will it be today, Warren, the usual?' she knew the best way to deal with him was to ignore his pathetic attempts at humour.

'Yes, short backsides, please.'

Jill sighed 'a short back and sides it is, sir'

His laugh sounded like a donkey braying with a bellyache, 'you're getting used to me, eh, learning my code?'

Jill gave a wan smile and reached for the electric clippers. She worked as quickly as possible without appearing to rush. At least there were no other customers before him. She paused briefly to glance at his head from different angles as if considering each stroke. She knew he was watching her every move in the mirror waiting to make his next quip.

At least this session would be shorter than usual. Most barbers confined their chat to the person in the chair whilst those waiting their turn sat quietly reading. Not so with Warren, he foisted himself on all within earshot, inflicting upon them the tired tales of his navy days and his claimed sexual prowess in days of yore.

'I used to come here when your dad ran this place, you know. Thirty-odd years I've been coming here ever since I left the Navy. I was almost as good looking then as I am now.' He winked and sniggered at his reflection as he always did when delivering this line.

Please, God, thought Jill, not this again. Every bloody time the old fart comes in it's the same tale.

"Yer dad always asked me if I wanted anything for the weekend, blah blah, you know, a packet of three, wink, wink. Barbers were about the only ones who sold condoms in the good old days" etc.

Jill tried to politely steer him away from his long boring monologue of yesteryear. She failed. Today, being in no mood to listen, she cut him off.

'Yes, Warren, you've told us all that before' she grinned broadly so as not to give offence 'Not losing yer marbles, are you mate?' Her laugh sounded almost convincing.

'Not lost anything, love' Warren said cheerfully, patting the front of his trousers suggestively, 'you ask my missus.' He leered into the mirror, his gimlet blue eyes sparkling in his turtle-like face, his ill-fitting dentures shone like a double row of bleached tombstones.

Jill felt her stomach lurch. The old boy had the knack of introducing sex into every topic of conversation, no matter how innocent. He'd turned it into an art form.

Jill coughed 'yes, well, pressing right on, Warren,' she said with a tired smile, desperate to get him onto a sex-free topic, 'are you going anywhere exciting for your holidays this year?'

Warren said 'well, I was thinking of going to Thailand, but the wife isn't into strip clubs these days and she doesn't want all those foreign birds after my body' he chortled 'We'll be going to Clacton-on-Sea

Sweet and Sour

for a week in June as usual.' He looked slyly across at June, undressing her with his eyes 'that would be good, eh? A week *in* June.' He thrust his hips forward, underlining his double entendre.

June's cream-curdling, glare caused Warren's face to sag, even he knew he'd gone too far. 'Not many strip clubs in Clacton' he ended lamely. A few moments of embarrassed silence followed.

Jill was, at last, coming to the end of his trim, the seven minutes it had taken seemed like an eternity to her. It was always the same with Warren, non-stop prattle, bad jokes and sexual innuendo. If her husband Bob knew he'd give the old boy a flea in his ear and send him packing. But June was probably right, he was just a dirty-minded but harmless old scrote and as mad as a barking duck. He always tipped well, though.

Warren arose from the chair, embarrassment quickly forgotten 'I suppose you're going to mention money now?' he said with mock shock 'and we were getting on so well, too.' It was what he always said on every visit.

'That'll be seven pounds, Warren, please.'

He withdrew his wallet and, as usual, produced a crisp ten-pound note and again, as usual, he said 'keep the change, love.'

Warren took his coat off the stand, and beamed at them both 'see ya soon, you sexy sirens.'

Both women knew that when he got to the door he'd turn and say, 'And if I can't get in next time, I'll send someone over with the money, OK?' Same old, same old.

Only this time he surprised them.

'Next time I come I'll have a big surprise for you girls.' he said in a low, conspiratorial tone 'the wife would go mad if she knew I've taken it out and shown you.'

Both women's eyebrows shot into their hairlines as their mouths fell open. It was June who recovered first, her suspicions spinning around her brain like demented dervish dancers. 'What the hell are you talking about?' she asked sharply.

Warren didn't pick up on her brusque tone, 'just you wait and see' he chirped throwing them a lecherous grin, 'I'll give you a clue, it's quite a big one and it shows its pleasure when stroked.' He turned before the shocked women could think of a reply and walked out of the shop whistling, a swagger in his step.

'Oh, God' said Jill as the door closed behind him, 'I hope I'm never alone in the shop when he calls, that old perv gives me the creeps.'

'He was one of daddy's best customers and he brought a lot of his mates here, too. I don't think we can ban him without losing a lot of customers. The other old boys seem to think the world of him.' June said her worried face reflecting Jill's thoughts. 'Has he finally lost it d'you think?'

*

The weeks passed and the incident sank into the morass of their daily routine. Short Backsides strange promise was all but forgotten. Business was slowly picking up again as Covid restrictions were further eased.

One quiet afternoon some weeks later June's phone buzzed. 'Oh dear, Jill, my old man has had an emergency call-out, I'll have to leave to pick the kids up from nursery, good job we're not busy.'

'OK, love, but please, try to be back for when the schools come out, we'll be busy then.'

*

June had been gone about ten minutes, Jill, all alone in the empty shop, was contemplating nipping out the back for a quick smoke when Warren barged in, his face beaning a wide, and even more inane grin than usual 'Hello Jill, me darlin' he said glancing slyly around the shop 'I've got you all to myself, have I?' Without waiting for an answer, he threw himself into her chair and spread his legs, 'short backsides, please' he quipped.

Jill nervously draped the cape around his skinny shoulders and, with trembling hands, tucked it into his collar. Warren shuddered with ecstasy 'Core, wonderful touch you have Jill, your old man's very lucky to have you seeing to him. His eyes narrowed; his usual lewd smile playing about his lips.

Jill sighed and, picking up the shears, began to work. She deliberately remained silent so as not to encourage him. Inwardly she prayed for another customer to call in but at two fifty-five on a wet Wednesday afternoon, it was highly improbable.

Warren's grin got wider but he said nothing, he just kept watching her in the mirror almost slavering with anticipation of some word or deed.

Jill finished her task and stood back.

'You'll remember last time I was here I told you I wanted to show you something special' Warren said, his tone dark and mysterious, 'well, it's right here, in my trousers.' He whipped the large barbers' cape aside.

Jill glanced down and noticed a long bulge extending from his groin down his left trouser leg. His hand slid, down and stroked it before he reached towards his waistband. Jill gasped in horror, her hands flying over her mouth, her electric shears clattering on the floor as she stared, transfixed.

Warren slowly undid his waistband and slid his zip down. 'Don't be afraid Jill, just slip your hand down here and give it a stroke, it won't bite.' his eyes twinkled brightly as his teeth showed their skeletal, white gleam, adding to the horror of the moment. He was enjoying himself.

Sweet and Sour

Jill screamed and recoiled; her eyes wide with fear.' What the hell are you doing, you crazy old sod?'

Warren got out of the chair and turned towards her, a gargoyle-like grin on his face 'don't be afraid love, it's not that big and it's very friendly, the wife loves it.' He thrust his hand deep into his trousers. He seemed to be having difficulty extracting it. 'Come to daddy' he muttered then at last his hand came free. 'This,' he announced, 'is Georgie-Porgy' and produced his wife's pet ferret. 'it's the only way I could smuggle him out, the wife would go daft if she knew.'

Jill gave a terrified shriek. All her life she'd had a fear of mice, rats, gerbils and guinea pigs. Being close to anything small and furry sent her into meltdown. Her eyes bulged as Georgie-Porgy's enquiring little nose came sniffing towards her, thrust forward by Warren. Jill screamed again, overwhelmed by panic. She grabbed the shop broom. 'Get it away from me. Get it away!'

Warren was shocked to his core, a bemused look on his face 'I thought you'd be pleased…'

Jill lashed out with the broom, hitting Warren's wrist and causing him to drop poor Georgie-Porgy. The frightened ferret took off as the hysterical hairdresser leapt onto the counter scattering clippers and combs in every direction, clutching her skirt to her thighs and shrieking at the top of her lungs.

At that moment, the prayed-for customer entered.

Seeing a terrified, screaming woman being confronted by an old man with his trousers wide open, off duty constable William Harper put two and two together and came up with five. 'You dirty old bugger' he roared and grabbed Warren, throwing him into a painful armlock and wrestling him to the floor.

'Not him. Not him, Jill shouted, pointing at Georgie-Porgy as he scuttled along the skirting board seeking a hiding place.

Harper left Warren and dived for the ferret which promptly turned around and ran under him back towards Warren. Seeing his chance, Warren grabbed the petrified creature and stuffed him hurriedly down his underpants.

Poor Georgy-Porgy was utterly confused by the din and the rough handling. Stuffed unceremoniously into the dark, smelly confines of Warren's Y-fronts he mistook the flabby wedding tackle for a hostile one-eyed ferret and sank his teeth deep into it.

Warren screamed, wild-eyed, and started doing a frantic jig, beside himself in pain and panic. Georgy-Porgy realising his enemy didn't taste of ferret, let go and dashed down Warren's trouser leg to make his escape.

Just then a lady with two young boys opened the door and stood gaping at the sight of a woman standing on the counter screaming, an old man with his trousers around his ankles clutching his codpiece

Sweet and Sour

and jumping up and down howling his head off. There was also another man on his hands and knees, his backside high in the air looking under the barber's chair crying, 'here ferret, ferret.'

The horrified lady hurriedly turned around and ushered her charges out, white-faced.

Georgie-Porgy seized his chance and dashed out of the shop and onto the main road. 'Noooo' cried Warren and, kicking off the encumbering trousers, dived after him. Harper leapt up and tried to stop him, but Warren was surprisingly nimble for his years. He slipped Harper's grasping hand and dashed out after his wife's beloved pet. Georgy-Porgy scampered across the main road, Warren charging after him in wild panic.

The bus driver braked hard swerving to avoid the arm-waving, trouserless lunatic who'd suddenly appeared from nowhere. This caused a terrified cyclist to be run off the road sending him careering across the pavement into a low garden wall where he flew, with a despairing wail, headfirst into some rose bushes.

Warren almost made it, but the offside of the bus brushed his buttocks spinning him like a top and sending him sliding across the tarmac where he received a severe dose of gravel rash. Gorgy-Porgy ran off home uninjured to the safety of his cage.

They lost Warren's custom for good that day.

The Resident Poet

Big bad Bob sashayed into the Biker bar. 'Evenin' y'all' he said to no one in particular then he burped, farted, and weaved his way to the bar.

'Hey, let's have a goddamn beer over here' he bawled. A beer appeared served by a nervous bar keep.

Bob looked around the bar room, everyone was talking easy, laughing, and enjoying their beer. This offended Bob. Hell, this was a biker bar, wasn't it? There should be trouble, shouldn't there? Then Bob noticed something that really boiled his piss. A skinny old guy sitting alone at the end of the bar quietly sucking on a Budweiser bottle.

'Who the hell let you in here old fart?' Bob yelled.

The old man glanced up then went back to his drink.

A guy at a nearby table volunteered 'That thar is 'ole Motor Mouth Mason our resident poet.'

'Resident fuckin' whut?' asked Bob incredulous, 'this a biker bar or a milk bar?'

Bob felt his bile rising, these guys looked like real deal bikers but, shit, poetry fer chrissakes? 'Whut y'all got goin' on next week, needle point? he asked unable to contain his contempt.

He ambled over to the poet. 'Hey ya old asshole let's hear some goddamned po'try, huh.'

Ole Motor Mouth simply took another sip from his beer.

Bob spun the old guy round on his stool and saw the poet's craggy face full on. It was ravaged by scars; one eye socket was empty, and half an ear was gone.

'Say, ya ole turd, how the fuck you git so goddamn ugly anyways?'

'A-fightin.'

You could have heard a pin drop. All attention was now riveted on the pair then the guy who'd spoke first said quietly 'I'd leave that ole boy alone if'n I was you, mistah.'

'Well, yah ain't me asshole so just shut the fuck up.'

The guy just smiled and raised his beer in salute.

'So, gimme some of yer shit-fer-brains po'try yah ole coot.'

'Don' think ah will 'til 'yuh 'pologise,

An' say purty-please, is what I'd advise'

This unexpected couplet stopped Bob for a second 'You sassin' me ole man?'

'Yes, son, guessin' ah am' the old man poked his tongue out.

Bob looked as happy as a vulture with fresh roadkill. He smirked at the barkeep then slowly and deliberately gripped Motor Mouth by his shirt front, pulling him half out of his seat.

The old guy's free hand shot out; splayed fingers rigid as he flew them into Bob's eyes with the speed of a striking rattler. Bob screamed in agony his hands flying to his face, his beer fell shattering, splattering foam across the floor. As he fell back a pace Motor Mouth's silver tipped biker boot flew up and out catching Bob squarely in the balls. Bob, folded faster than a bad poker hand, gagging and puking.

When Bob subsided into a moaning heap, Motor Mouth turned, pointed to his face and addressed the saloon:

'The reason I'm a-wearin' all these scars
Ain't frum fightin' in brothels and bars
But takin' on the enemies of our land
That still abound on every hand
To earn the right fer Bob an' y'all
Nasty names fer me t'call
In peace an' freedom like you'd expect
So just show us old guys some respect
Cos if'n I got t' git offa this stool
Well, folks, I might jus' lose mah cool
Then boys y'all can bet yer shirt
Some bastard here's gonna git bad hurt
So, git this sorry ass outta here
Oh, an' before ya do, he owes me a beer.

Sweet and Sour

The bar exploded in wild applause and ole Motor Mouth Mason ('Nam vet, Silver Star and resident poet) didn't buy another beer for a month.

Don' y'all jus' love a happy ending?

Snakes and Ladders

There I was folks, pretending I was mowing my lawn to keep an eye on our window cleaner. He's a lazy sod who never cleans into the corners. The mower suddenly stopped, and I stared down at it non-plussed. The cable supplying the mower had somehow managed to get itself caught under the blades, the ragged ends thrown behind me.

I was confused for a moment and stood scratching my head. Stepping back from my dead machine I stood on the live shredded cable. There was a flash and a bang, the shock sent me crashing into the window cleaner's ladder. He let out a sort of strangled yelp and sailed over the garden fence his arms flailing wildly.

Talk about good luck, his fall was broken by the roof of my neighbor's greenhouse; well, the lad had a few lacerations, but nothing that a blood transfusion wouldn't cure.

Now my neighbour John, he's a bit of a humourless git, he came out to see what was happening. He went crazy at the window cleaner 'cos he'd flattened his best tomato plants and squashed all the tomatoes he was showing that weekend at the harvest festival show. John has won first prize these

Sweet and Sour

last three years and was expecting to do it again. I think it was that that might have upset him a bit.

'Bloody sabotage' he yelled and started jumping up and down, by God he was fair spitting feathers. He grabbed a plant pot and started clouting the window cleaner around the head. The poor lad was crying and wailing and trying to explain it weren't his fault. I tried to say something, but John wasn't listening. I grabbed one of his broken bamboo tomato poles and give John a swift jab in the buttocks just to get his attention. I'm not a gardener, how heck was I to know broken bamboo is razor-sharp? I wasn't being nasty.

Ah said 'Now then John lad, don't take on so, you can always fry them tomatoes up for breakfast.' Well, I was only trying to be helpful, there was no need to thump me too. Good job it was only a plastic plant pot.

All this noise and kerfuffle attracted the attention of the missus who, up 'til that time, had been quietly knitting me a willie warmer for Christmas out of an old ball of string she'd found on the rubbish tip.

'What the 'ell's happening here?' says she, picking up the mower wire and walking through the broken fence.

When she saw the window cleaner laying in the greenhouse covered in blood, she remembered doing first aid years ago.' Hold that a minute' she said, handing John the wire.

There was a big blue flash, and John went flying through his garage window and knocked over a big pillar drill that fell off the bench and landed with an almighty bang on the bonnet of the vintage car he'd just finished restoring.

The missus stood staring with her gob open for a second then whacked me around the ear as hard as she could. 'What the hell was that for?' I wailed.

'That could have been me yer feckless owd fool' she snapped 'you should have switched the power off.'

John's piercing scream caused his wife Joan to leave her ironing and dash downstairs to see what was going on. She screamed and ran into the garage to where John was on his knees clutching his broken ribs and looking at his vintage car. He was sobbing hysterically for some reason; some folks are very easily upset you know.

I thought the window cleaner had better take the rest of the day off and maybe have the ambulance folk look him over to be on the safe side, so I went into the house to ring 'em. As I was ringing 'em I noticed smoke pouring out of an upstairs window in John's house. I said, 'Oh, and can you send the fire brigade as well please, next door seems to be afire.'

When Joan had heard John screaming, she'd dived downstairs from her workroom, but she'd left a nylon shirt on the end of the ironing board. It had slipped off onto an electric fire.

Sweet and Sour

I must say the emergency services were there quickly. Whilst the ambulance folk were applying pressure to the window cleaner's scratches, sorting the slight compound fracture of his left femur and getting a drip into him the firefighters turned up.

Not one's for talking first and acting later those fire lads. John's front door was locked so they took an axe to it and battered it down to run in a hose. It was a real pity 'cos the front door was, brand new and made from solid polished oak. I believe it had cost John and Joan over fifteen hundred pounds just the week before, shame really.

I watched the firefighters until they came out of John's house again and the guy at the fire engine shut the pump down. I was proper impressed with the speed they'd sorted the fire, so I run across to tell 'em. Now, unfortunately, in my enthusiasm to deliver my praise and admiration, I tripped over the damned fire hose and went arse over tit into the lad controlling the pump. He shot his hand out to save himself as we fell, and his hand caught the pump lever.

Lots of things went wrong all at once after that. The fire engine's revs went berserk, the laid down hosepipe instantly filled with water which shot out of the end soaking the firefighters and causing the hoses to whiplash wildly like giant snakes gone mad.

Now, this wouldn't have been too bad as it only knocked a couple of firemen off their feet. However, the paramedics chose that very moment to appear around the side of John's house wheeling the window cleaner down the rather steep drive to the ambulance. He was OK because he was strapped on tight. to the stretcher, gurney thingy.

The hose took the legs from under the lady pushing the damn gurney thingy and off it shot down the drive with the window cleaner screaming his head off. Again, he had incredibly good luck as the bus driver saw him just in time and managed to swerve across the road missing him by inches. Unfortunately, he hit the ambulance, shunting it into the fire engine with a hell of a bang. The bus driver was leaning out of his window shouting to me, but I didn't have my hearing aids in. Anyway, I don't know a bar steward called Billy.

Fortunately for the window cleaner, the gurney stopped when it hit the curbstone on the opposite side of the road and tipped up on its end. I found out later that the lad didn't have a fractured skull before that happened but, hey, you can't be lucky all the time.

At this point, the ambulance woman was wailing because her ankle was broken, the Firemen were screaming murder trying to capture their hoses, and the poor fireman I knocked over is sitting dazed on the pavement nursing his head. People are staggering off the bus clutching various body parts and moaning. As the police turned up it all got a bit too much for me and our lass. We ran into the house and hid under the bed 'til the shouting died down and the bus

Sweet and Sour

passengers had been treated by the fleet of ambulances that attended.

Later, I said to the policeman taking the statement 'it was damn lucky the ambulance was already there because the paramedic lady had her broken ankle seen to straight away.'

John and Joan's house was in a bit of a state. The smoke had damaged their decorating which he'd just had done, and the water ruined the bedroom carpet. It also brought down the kitchen ceiling and wrecked their nice kitchen units as well as completely shorting out their electrical system.

We did offer to put them up for the night, but they refused, muttering something about they'd feel safer sleeping in a minefield. An extremely harsh attitude I thought.

The media exaggerated the whole affair as usual saying that damage amounting to half a million pounds had been done and not all compensation claims were in yet.

And now I've no one to clean my windows or mow my lawn. Do you fancy a job this weekend?

The Ramsbottom Riots

'I want to go on the steam train from Bury to Rawtenstall this weekend' said the missus out of the blue.

'Why?' I asked, 'what's there?'

'Nowt much, but I want to stop off at Ramsbottom' said she, 'they have a great Sunday market.'

So that Sunday off we went. I hate traipsing around markets but she who passeth all understanding says we're going, so I go. Anything for a quiet life.

After two hours traipsing around Ramsbottom market, my arthritic hip was killing me, so I bought a golf brolly that would double as a walking stick. All was well until we went to reboard the train. We joined the queue and waited. My hip throbbed so I put the brolly down and leant on it.

There came a piercing shriek right down my hearing aid, I damn near jumped out of my skin. I'd put the brolly on the woman's foot behind me. She was jumping up and down 'Me toe, oh, oh, me toe,' she wailed.

I felt sorry the lass and tried to cheer her up by making a little joke. 'Never mind, lass,' I quipped, you've got another nine toes.'

Oh, how I wish I hadn't said it. Her husband was not impressed. 'Funny bugger, eh?' he said and swiped me around the head with his brolly 'Let's hear you laugh that off pal.'

I was dazed, he'd damn near switched my lights off, but I recovered and fetched him one with my brolly. Next thing I know we're swinging like two knights of old, sword fighting. His wife was hopping on one foot pounding my back screaming 'leave him alone, leave him alone.'

I couldn't leave him alone or I'll get another whack. My missus is shouting 'Give over yer daft owd sods.' A crowd gathers around cheering. I'm desperate now and blowing like a breaching whale. He's not doing so well either, he was puce in the face and struggling for breath. I decided to duck his next blow and come up with my brolly point into his guts like a soldier with a rifle and bayonet.

He swung. I ducked. He hits his missus square in the chops with a meaty thwack! Her false teeth flew out and landed in the road just in time to be crushed to powder a passing taxi. I came up with my brolly and caught him in the guts. Down he goes like a deflated bouncy castle.

The bloke's missus screams and hops around to help him up. She reaches down just as he pukes all over her feet. The crowd go wild laughing and clapping as the station master walked up. 'You' he said, pointing at me.

'Me, mate?'

'Yes, you mate. Clear off, you're a troublemaker, you're not getting on this train.'

'But…. But, 'says I.

'But me no buts' says he 'begone or I'll fetch the police.'

So, aggrieved and getting earache from the missus we departed. I wasn't down for long though, being one of life's enthusiastic folk.

*

The Train leaves Ramsbottom station directly over the main road. It was hissing merrily away at the platform and the road barriers were down. I said to the missus, 'let's go and watch it leave from the barrier.' So, off we went.

All was peaceful and bucolic as we stood leaning on the barrier rail. A lady with a little dog came up and she and the missus started chatting. A girl on a horse rode up and stopped. After a minute a bloke drove up in a posh car stopped behind the horse and then another car followed by a motorcycle. I like motorbikes so I went to have a look at this brand-new Kawasaki. I was about to make an admiring comment when the rider turned his head away, shoving his nose in the air.

Oh, I thought, stuck up sod, eh? Too grand to speak to a poor pensioner, are we? I thought I'd bring him down a peg or two, so I said 'who foisted this bag

Sweet and Sour

o' bolts on you then, eh? God, he must have been some salesman. I'd be upset if I won one of these.'

He took umbrage and shot to the front of the queue beside the horse ready for a quick getaway.

I returned to the missus, but the motorcyclist glowered at me from under the horse's, neck and revved the bike fiercely. This frightened the poor horse and it kicked out backwards breaking the headlamp of the posh car behind.

The motorist leapt out and started berating the young girl rider. The dog lady jumped to her defence 'Here, hold my dog' she said, handing me the lead.

Off she went to explain to the driver what had happened. 'Mind yer own damned business' he shouted and was most aggressive.

'Poor woman. I'm not having that' says my missus and goes over to join the dog lady. Well, blow me down if this bloke didn't start having a go at my wife, too. He was bawling, waving his fist and getting right out of order. The dog was leaping up and down and barking like mad, straining at the lead to be defending her owner. I tied it to some handy railings and went across.

'And you can eff off, too, yer owd fart' he screamed at me.

Now, I've always believed that a demonstration is far better than an explanation. So, gripping him firmly by the gizzard and the goolies, I coaxed him gently back into his car where he sagged gagging and nursing his nuts but otherwise unharmed.

During this altercation, the motorcyclist did a rapid U-turn to the back of the queue out of the way, the snivelling little git.

I turned back to the barrier. Oh, woe. The train had left during the row. All I got to see was the last two carriages passing rapidly by.

The little dog suddenly went quiet, but its owner started screaming 'Me Fanny, oh, oh, me little Fanny.'

I'd inadvertently tied the dog to the level crossing barrier rails, and Fanny was dangling ten feet in the air kicking like mad and making horrible choking noises.

The guy in the signal box saw the unfortunate hound wafting past his window and rapidly lowered the barrier again.

A lot of things went awfully wrong after that.

The girl on the horse was in the middle of the crossing and the irate motorist was moving off as the barrier came down straight through his windscreen. The idiot on the motorbike decided he'd race down the outside of the queue and clear off sharpish.

Bang! He went face-first into the barrier, flying off the back of his machine which fell and skidded across the crossing. The petrol cap came off spilling fuel and the sparks flying from the dragging footrest set it alight.

Whoosh! It went up next to the horse which reared up and took off down the line after the train, the girl hanging around its neck shrieking for help.

The poor lad in the signal box was staring down in pale-faced horror, clutching his head and gasping for breath. The dog lady was crouched down howling hysterically and hugging her hound.

The motorist lost the plot completely. He dived out of his car and started kicking seven bells out of the motorbike lad who was wailing and holding up his hands.

All this kerfuffle brought the lads out of the pub where they had been watching a football match. They stood around, pints in hand, watching the action some cheering some jeering. Then a harsh word was spoken, and some silly bugger threw a punch. Oh, my god, it all kicked off then. The bike continued to blaze in the centre of the road. The stopped traffic started a horn blaring contest, the brawling blokes were belting the bejaysus out of one another in the middle of the street. And a crowd of open mouthed on-lookers gathered. Kids wailed and mothers moaned.

'Well, bless my soul' said the missus, 'I'm glad I don't live here, this place is chaotic.'

In the distance I saw blue lights flashing and heard sirens screaming. The riot police were coming. 'I wonder what started it all off?' I said.

'I dunno' she said, scratching her head, 'it beats me.'

We slipped surreptitiously away and caught the bus home.

It made the local news, of course. They dubbed it the Ramsbottom riots. Typical media nonsense. They also said the police were looking for an older couple to help with their enquiries.

I don't think we'll be going back there for a while.

Pooh Sticks

Terrence and Tina Townsend were walking around Hollingworth lake with their twin children Tuck and Tanya. All was fun and frolics until they came upon on a bridge over a gently flowing stream.

'Oh daddy, look' cried the eight-year-olds in unison 'can we play pooh sticks? Please daddy, please.' Terence smiled as broadly as a benevolent bishop bestowing a benediction and broke a couple of dead twigs from a nearby bush. 'Here you are my darlings.' They ran nudging each other and giggling, each vying to be first to the bridge. Upon reaching the parapet they realised it was far too high for them to see over it.

Terrence and Tina lifted their children up to the coping stones and let them lean over. 'Wait for it' said Tina 'three, two, one, go!' The twigs were released as were the wriggling children who ran excited to the other side and raised their arms to be lifted.

They were waiting excitedly for the first twig to appear when they were interrupted by a squeaky but somewhat authoritarian voice. 'Excuse me, may I have a word?'

Terrence and Tina turned to see a portly person parading towards them, his corpulent belly swaying ponderously before him. He was dressed in an oversized pink high-vis jacket above which was precariously perched a pink safety helmet. He glanced from the family to his clipboard as he advanced. The children were lowered and ceased giggling as the family politely waited for him to speak.

Drawing himself up to his full five-foot four-inch height the stranger said, 'may I ask exactly what activity you're involved in here?'

Terrence inwardly bristled at the man's pomposity but thought it best to be polite. 'We are sir, letting our children play pooh sticks.'

'I see' the man said, frowning as he made a note on his clipboard.

'And just who might you be, sir?' asked Tina,

'I am' said the man, pausing for dramatic effect, 'Mr. Percival Payne, the council's Chief Environmental Safety Officer. He flourished his ID card fussily. Then this epitome of pomposity pronounced peremptorily 'I believe, sir, that you are engaged in activities which contravene several of the Local Authorities codes of countryside conduct.

Terrence's normally friendly face sagged in slack-jawed disbelief, 'we are allowing our children to play an innocent game of pooh sticks, man.' Terrence then smiled and surveyed the surrounding fields 'OK, so where's the hidden camera, mate? This is one of those TV wind-ups, yeah?'

Percy put his fist to his mouth and affected a throat-clearing cough. He composed his fat face and triple chin into what he fondly imagined was a stern authoritarian look. 'I'm afraid this is no joking matter, sir. I have observed you damaging a tree and putting minors at risk twice by elevating them to an inappropriate position.' Percy peered petulantly over his safety spectacles 'May I ask if you carried out a full risk assessment before commencing this ill-advised adventure, sir?'

Terrence and Tina were dumbstruck. At last Terrence, blinking and bemused, managed 'a what mate?'

'Clearly, there are major safety implications here' continued Payne, ignoring Terrence's question. 'To begin with, it is required under bye-law 2702, paragraph 13, subsection iv that minors wear high-visibility vests at all times when participating in outdoor pursuits in council-controlled countryside' he took a deep breath. 'Secondly: when engaging in these arduous adventurous activities minors should be equipped with safety helmets, harnesses, floatation devices and any other approved safety equipment required by the said activity.' Percy paused, glancing at his clipboard as he ticked several boxes with the punctilious air of a comic opera clown.

Seeing Tina about to speak Percy held up a pudgy hand to indicate there was more to come. 'Furthermore,' he continued, 'you allowed these minors to run unescorted and unsupervised across the highway contrary to section 84 paragraph 147 sub-clause 89 amendment 12 of the highways and byways act.'

'But it's only an empty bridle path barely fourteen feet wide' protested Tina, too gobsmacked even to feel angry.

'That is as maybe madam' said Percy, 'but it still constitutes a highway for purposes of environmental health and safety.' He glanced again at his clipboard checking his notes. 'Now, we come to the matter of criminal damage to the tree Mr. er...er...?

'What on earth are you talking about, man?'

'Those branches you tore off that bush, sir.'

'Oh, you mean the two dead twigs?' said Terrence, sidestepping the oblique request for his name 'I'll report it to the *branch* manager' he quipped, trying to inject a little humour into the bizarre situation. It fell flat.

'Bye-law 1013a of 1972, chapter 41, paragraph 19, sub-paragraph vii states categorically that under no circumstances may any tree, bush, shrub, plant or herb be pruned, cut, transplanted, carried away or otherwise molested unless written permission from the Parks and Recreational Invigilating Committee (PRIC) is first obtained.' Percy hovered, his pen

Sweet and Sour

poised expectantly above his clipboard 'I'll need your full names and address for my report' he said.

Terrence, a mild-mannered man, finally snapped 'you ain't having them, mate' he growled belligerently. 'For a start, you've upset my family with your pathetic petty persecution. That, Percy, is contrary to Parental Practices for Pleasurable Pursuits Protocol, chapter 19 paragraph 197 sub-clause 17 bloody B' he bawled, his frustration rising rapidly. 'Secondly: If you don't piss off and leave us alone, I'll wedge my non-standard, unapproved, size 10 walking boot so hard up your fat arse the shock will make your eyes bleed.'

Percy paled 'I shall have to report this unwarranted threat of physical violence to the appropriate authorities immediately.' He produced his phone. 'Oh, dear, I haven't got a signal, I shall have to commandeer yours' he said, holding out his hand.

*

Percy Payne plodded painfully into the council meeting, his haemorrhoids hurting him horribly, to recite his recommendations.

At the cost of £25,012.40 to the local taxpayers, the council erected an anti-pooh sticks fence at the upstream end of the bridge. They daubed the apexed parapet with anti-climb paint with warning signs prominently displayed. They also placed garish green notice boards at regular intervals along the path to warn people not to lean over the bridge.

"Danger deep water" signs were erected, and lifebelts provided either side of the stream to the amusement of the local vandals. The stream was only one foot ten inches deep, but the signs had been deemed necessary because in the spring of 1948, due to a huge snowmelt, the stream had reached a depth of three feet eight inches.

*

Poor Percival Payne died in tragic circumstances. He was found lying face down in the stream under the pooh sticks bridge smeared in anti-climb paint. He had neck injuries consistent with a fall. The likeliest explanation for his demise was that he, being a very conscientious Environmental Safety Officer, had been testing the effectiveness of his safety measures when he slipped and fell. The coroner, however, returned an open verdict because no adequate explanation could be found as to why a large twig was protruding from Percy's anus.

Wild Sex and Weddings

Have you ever noticed that there's a 'spare uncle' in almost every group photo of a sixties or seventies wedding?

He is the little man on the end, grinning inanely into the camera. His jacket cuffs overhang his knuckles and his wrinkled trousers sag over his down-at-heel shoes. A nylon shirt with a fly-away collar and an ill-matched tie usually completes this ensemble. There is every chance this epitome of sartorial inelegance is my late Uncle Eddie, bus driver and weekend wedding crasher.

Eddie, a committed bachelor, carefully researched the wedding announcements every week looking for large working-class weddings. He'd buy the appropriate buttonhole, turning up a minute or two before the service started. Nodding shy hellos, he'd take a back pew. No one wanted to cause embarrassment by asking who he was, each family assuming he belonged to the other.

At the reception, Eddie would seek out the unpopular maiden aunt. (There's always one) She's the oddball who must be invited for family reasons. He would tell her a couple of jokes then spin her a yarn of a lost wallet to scrounge free drinks. The poor wallflower, flattered by his attention and recognising a kindred spirit, willing paid.

If questioned as to his identity, which rarely happened, Eddie would look bemused, scratch his ear, and say 'well, this is where my carers dropped me off.'

They'd call a taxi, give him a slice of wedding cake, and send him home, shaking their heads sympathetically.

As Eddie's confidence grew, he decided to up his game and crash a posh wedding. There he met the wonderful Wilhelmina, a huge but perfectly proportioned lady dressed more garishly than Donald Trump's Christmas tree. She was displaying Grand Canyon cleavage and a come-hither smile. Unknown to Eddie, Wilhelmina, had an agenda.

After a couple of glasses of champagne and a plateful of canapes, she placed her hand on his thigh, stroking suggestively. She whispered, 'I have a room here, Eddie, dearest, and I need sex. So, how about it, eh?'

Eddie's eyebrows hit his hairline and his eyes bulged as a wave of terror engulf him. His only experience of sex was a fumble with Doris Dodds behind the bike shed at school. They had been caught by Mrs Hardaker the R.E teacher. She had shrieked so loudly that Eddie ran off screaming, desperately trying to pull his trousers up from around his knees. He tripped and fell in the playground, hapless lad, exposing his bare backside before the whole school. Deeply traumatized, Eddie never tried sex again.

'Er…oh…righto' he stammered 'I'll…I'll just have to nip to the gents first.'

Eddie's narrow shoulders went through the toilet window easily enough, but his bulbous backside got wedged. His short fat legs were kicking frantically when Wilhelmina caught up with him. Grabbing his waistband, she unfastened his belt and slid his pants, Y-fronts, and slip-on shoes off in one deft movement. Taking him by the tackle she drew him back in screaming.

Wilhelmina pushed him into a cubicle still firmly gripping his family heirlooms, her free hand clamped over his mouth. 'Listen, Eddie, I know you're a gate crasher' she said, her eyes dark with lust. 'Do as you're told, my dear, and I'll not tell that big nephew of mine to thump you and throw you bare-arsed into the street.'

A petrified Eddie meekly obeyed and was led, re-clothed and trembling to Wilhelmina's room.

The sex was a revelation to Eddie as Wilhelmina demonstrated the pleasures an experienced woman could give a man. He wept tears of joy as she insisted on doing it again and again until both were exhausted.

Over breakfast in their room, Wilhelmina dropped her bombshell. 'Eddie, I knew what you were up to because I'm doing it myself' she said, grinning like a split watermelon. 'This time I'm a long-lost cousin who emigrated to Australia and who just happened to be in the country on holiday.'

Eddie's jaw dropped 'and that big nephew?'

'Don't know him from Adam, Eddie, that was just a ploy to bed you.'

Eddie gasped. 'Good god, gate-crashing's a bit risky for a lone woman, ain't it?'

Wilhelmina threw her head back and loosed a great guffaw, her big breasts jiggling like frolicking puppies. 'Risky? Not at all! Weddings are always cheerful events with lots of good food and booze.' She winked, 'and there's always a spare uncle who's up for a shag. It's ideal for a lusty lass like me.'

Both laughed so loud and long the people in the adjoining room banged on the wall. Over the next hour, they happily swapped stories of their escapades then she reached for him. 'Time for a quickie before checking out time, Eddie, whaddya say?'

Eddie and Wilhelmina became firm friends, joining forces to crash weddings as a "respectable" couple. In 1976, after a year of wild sex and weddings, they got married in a lavish ceremony with friends and relatives coming from far and wide. It was a sunny, blissful occasion with champagne and bonhomie flowing freely.

A week later, browsing the wedding photos, they were surprised to see an innocuous little man in an ill-fitting suit on the edge of the group. Shocked, they pointed, simultaneously asking 'who the hell's that?' Then they collapsed in peels of hysterical laughter.

Mighty Military Magic

The biggest bully boy in our gun Battery was a large lumpen lout of Scottish origin known as Horrible Hamish. He spat in my brother David's beer one night in the NAAFI* 'Whit ye gonna do aboot that, shitheed?' he asked.

David looked at his oppressor and smiled 'you can buy me another pint and be forgiven, Hamish, otherwise it's the watch-your-step curse.'

'Awa' tae fuck ye wee gobshite afore ah twat ye.'

'OK' said David calmly 'have it your way, Hamish. The watch-your-step curse it is, then.' He left the pint and walked out.

Hamish's lips curled in a contemptuous sneer. 'Ye're a fookin' pooftah.'

Slight of frame, blonde of mane and fair of face, he walked with grace did my brother David. He was not cut out to be a soldier, and it showed. Certain civilian gentlemen oft-made advances that he skilfully rejected. David wasn't good just looking, he was beautiful. Witty quips readily fell from his full lips, which got him into trouble with the slow-minded bully boys and with those in authority over him.

David was forced to find ways of defending himself from the bully boys his overly mobile mouth inevitably attracted. He put it around that he could cast magic spells and that people who crossed him suddenly got very unlucky. The first response was, as expected, ridicule. David kept on smiling.

*

Pay night: Horrible Hamish got paralytic as usual and had to be carried to bed. At three a.m. David crept into his billet and slipped Hamish's brand-new expensive watch off his wrist. He levered the back off with his jackknife then filled the workings with glue. He wiped it clean and replaced it. He also replaced Hamish's army issue foot powder with an identical tin he'd made up then sprinkled a little powdered bleach into the toes of his victim's socks. The whole operation took less than five minutes.

The next day we went on a route march. Nothing too strenuous, just a twenty miler.

After three miles, Hamish began to hobble. After seven miles he fell behind, at ten he was almost crying with pain as the sweat-activated bleach burned his tootsies. He was dropping further and further behind to the annoyance of Battery Sergeant Major Robert (Gobby) Hobbie, aka Bob-the-Gob.

'What the hell's up with yer?' bawled Gobby, 'yer walking like a wounded whore, whining like one, too.' He had a way with words did our Bob.

'It's ma feet surr' Hamish wailed 'they're on fire.'

'I'll set yer bleedin' arse on fire if you don't catch up' screamed Hobbie. Always ready to offer a word of encouragement was our BSM.

At fifteen miles Hamish was collapsed at the side of the road his boots and socks beside him. His feet were skinned and red raw. Even Bob stopped shouting when he saw them. I approach and asked, 'what time is it, Hamish?'

He pulled his sleeve back and glanced at his pride and joy 'Oh God, the bloody thing's stopped.'

'Ah,' I said solemnly 'that's the watch your step curse for sure. You'd best apologise to my brother and buy him a pint, or it could get worse.'

Hamish was in agony and in no mood for listening 'bollocks, Sarge' he said, 'Ah'll no be buying that wee twat onything.'

'Suit yourself' said I 'better watch your step, though' with that, I marched on leaving him to the following medics. They misdiagnosed it as severe athlete's foot and advised him to wash his feet frequently, dry them thoroughly, and make sure to use plenty of foot powder. David's replacement foot powder was fifty per cent powdered bleach. After a week of his condition steadily worsening, Hamish hobbled over to David in the NAAFI with a pint and an apology.

'Will ye no tak this bloody spell aff of me David?'

'Sure' said David 'but spells are easier to put on than take off, it'll cost.'

Sweet and Sour

A deal was struck, and David said he'd make some magic powder that would release the spell. He nipped to the local chemist and bought some potassium permanganate. Then he acquired some sugar from the cookhouse. A large bucket of scalding water was produced, and the scene was set. A crowd of eager gunners gathered around to watch the spell.

David lit a candle and sat cross-legged on the barrack room floor muttering a magical incantation, which consisted of a mixture of altar boy Latin and German swear words.

He stirred the bucket with a spoon as he incanted, slowly pouring in his "magic" powder. Hamish and the crowd watched in awe as the powder dissolved, swirling and billowing in exotic clouds, turning the water a deep violet colour. David kept on chanting to distract the on-lookers. He slipped a small amount of potassium permanganate and refined sugar into his hand.

Leaning over the bucket he rubbed his hands briskly together. The compound burst into flames and David let out a mighty roar plunging his hands rapidly into and out of the water, extinguishing the flames.

Hamish let out a terrified squawk and tried to do a runner, but David had briefed two burly helpers. They grabbed the injured man and buried his feet in the bucket. Hamish howled, the lads jeered and cheered. David was enjoying himself.

'Oh, Jesus, David' gasped Hamish upon his release, 'am I cured the noo?'

A stern-faced David and shook his head solemnly. 'No, not yet Hamish. Wait until the water cools and soak your feet for two hours. Tomorrow, the same ritual but with iced water, OK?' David gave him a fresh tin of Army issue foot powder 'use this from now on Hamish, I've blessed it. Throw the other one away, it's been cursed.'

The next day, after the same ritual was performed before an even bigger crowd, David declared the spell lifted and Hamish would start to heal.

'Sorry about the watch mate it, reversing only works on human beings.' Hamish healed, and David's reputation was sealed.

*

The sand in the Battery's Vaseline was Gobby Hobbie. Passed over for promotion, he loved making the gunners' lives a misery. The lads asked David to do something about him. 'I'll think on it.' was all he would say.

David's chance came a week later whilst we were out on manoeuvres. He went to the field kitchen for his dinner only to be confronted by Gobby. 'Your hands are filthy, gunner. Bugger off and clean them. And I mean clean' he bawled.

'But I've been working with graphite grease, sir. It's very difficult to remove, sir.'

Sweet and Sour

'You've got ten minutes.' snapped the unrelenting Gobby, 'Move yer arse.'

As part of his defence strategy, David had cultivated friends in low places, foremost of which was Bombardier 'Greasy' Grice, the Battery's biggest bullshitter, 'sod off to his tent, David. Use the bugger's toothbrush' he advised, 'I've done it myself before now.'

. So, David sneaked into Gobby's tent and rescued his toothbrush, scrubbing his hands and fingernails clean with it. David then saw some nearby animal droppings which gave him an idea. He dipped the toothbrush into the dried dung, shaking off the excess before replacing it. With the help of some spit, he smeared a fine film of it in Gobby's tin mug and around the rim of his water bottle.

When he got back to the field kitchen David's dinner was cold. Foolishly, he mentioned it to Gobby.

'Hot's a bonus lad, it's fuel, get it down yer neck and stop whingeing.' Gobby's eyes narrowed spitefully, 'and stay behind when you've finished, you're on cookhouse fatigues.'

David told the lads he'd cast a tummy bug spell on Gobby and to see what the next twenty-four hours brought. Sure enough, the next afternoon, Gobby went down with volatile vomiting and severe diarrhoea.

An hour later Gobby was gone, and peace reigned.

*

After returning to camp the lads were sitting in the NAAFI* drinking David's health and rejoicing at Gobby's misfortune. The BSM was off work for a week to everyone's great relief.

The men were also bemoaning the fact that none of them could get off with Theresa, the fittest NAAFI girl they'd ever had, 'she must be a lesbian' declared Horrible Hamish to a sea of nodding heads. Like most soldiers, each considered himself to be God's gift to women.

Theresa had sensibly turned down every advance with the same harsh words 'Yer only after one thing, yer randy bugger' she was right, too.

'I'll get a date with her' declared David 'give me a week.'

'Yeah, right, good luck with that mate' said Gunner "Goddo" Gonelly, the Battery's most rampant Romeo and successful seducer, 'pigs might fly.'

The week passed, those who had bet money on the outcome waited anxiously. David made sure he was seen escorting Theresa back to her quarters.

'How the hell did you manage to get off with her David?' All wanted to know his secret as the magician collected his winnings.

'Love spell, of course.'

David sold a dozen "love spells" at thirty shillings each to gobsmacked gunners. 'They only work if you follow the seven golden rules exactly' he told the gullible gits. 'Break just one of these rules and yer buggered. No money back.' He made each customer write the rules down.

Rule 1. You must recite the spell for a day then ask for a date respectfully.

Rule 2. On the way to the date, you must repeat the spell in your head while smiling.

Rule 3. Turn up on time and smartly dressed.

Rule 4. No groping, swearing, dirty jokes, getting drunk or bragging.

Rule 5. Take flowers, treat her to a meal and/or the cinema, then walk her home. Only kiss her good night if she wants you to. Only then ask for a second date.

Rule 6. Repeat the spell constantly on the way back to barracks.

Rule 7. Always believe in the spell and yourself. Doubt is deadly.

Unsurprisingly, there were several reports of great results and David was inundated with eager buyers.

'Go on then, brother, how did you pull it off?' I asked.

He smiled slyly, 'I told her I was gay, of course, and that I just wanted an understanding friend to talk to.'

'And she believed you?' I asked astonished.

He grinned so broadly I thought his face would split in half. 'Yes,' he said, 'a lot of people think I am gay anyway because of my looks.'

After a couple of platonic dates, he intimated that her beauty and sweet personality was curing him of his 'gayness.'

The silly girl believed the crafty little bugger and David spent a lot of nights in her room just being "cured."

· *NAAFI: Navy, Army, and Airforce Institute*

Guilt and Gullibility

Postmaster Silas Sligh loved his second-string job as his historic village's tour guide. The parish council paid him, and the tourists tipped him.

He was showing a large group of tourists around his picturesque village. They did the Norman church, the village stocks and the street of old thatched cottages. Cameras clicked and questions were asked, which were knowledgeably answered.

An hour later, making their way to the sixteenth-century pub, the group came across Barnaby. He was sitting outside the post office licking an ice cream cornet. His eyes held a vacant look under his dark mop which looked like it had been trimmed with a knife and fork. 'And this is Barnaby,' said Silas. 'He's a simple, harmless soul who always tells the truth, which can be hilarious at times.'

As a demonstration of Barnaby's honesty, the guide said, 'tell the folks how long your willie is, Barnaby?'

'Nine inches' said the youth enthusiastically, 'you wanna see it?' He put his hand to his flies.

The crowd laughed as Sligh vigorously waved away the offer 'No thanks, Barnaby, we'll take your word for it, we know you never tell lies.'

'No, I never tells lies, folks, it's naughty you see' beamed Barnaby at the crowd.

Warming to his task, the guide said, 'now watch this.' He produced a one-pound coin and a fifty pence piece. 'Here, Barnaby, which of these two coins do you want?'

Barnaby examined the coins carefully, his forefinger on his chin. 'Oh, this one, please' he said pocketing the fifty pence coin.

'Why that one Barnaby?'

Barnaby gave an inane laugh 'Tis the biggest one and it's the shiniest, too.'

The tourists tittered and produced coins of their own. Barnaby, confusion on his innocent face, always took the coin of least value.

Leaning against the post office wall were two bicycles. 'Just watch this,' Silas said, 'I received a brand-new bicycle this very morning and I still have the old worn-out one.' He presented the bikes with a showman's flourish. 'Now then, Barnaby' he said with a wink at the crowd, 'you can choose one of these bikes and keep it forever.'

'Really?' said Barnaby his eyes twinkling. He gave a lop-sided grin to the assembly 'Oi can ride a bike yer knows' he announced proudly, thrusting out his chest.

Sweet and Sour

'This one is brand new, Barnaby, but the old one is used to being ridden and is used to the lanes around here 'cos it's the one I used to deliver the mail.'

'Oh Arrh?' said the simpleton 'that'll be the one for me then.' He promptly mounted the machine and rode it around the village green waving madly to the laughing tourists, both hands off the handlebars. So keen to show off was he that he took his eye off where he was going. Barnaby hit a kerbstone causing him to wobble furiously and cry out in panic before pitching headlong into the village pond.

The tourists fell about laughing as Barnaby emerged coughing and spluttering with waterweed clinging to his hair like Neptune's toupee. But all appeared well as he held the bike aloft crying 'I is OK, folks, an' I could do with a bath anyways.'

The laughing group continued their way as a bedraggled Barnaby limped home to change.

*

After a pub lunch, the tourists were free to wander. Seeing Barnaby alone, one guilt-ridden tourist approached him. She felt the need to apologise for having taken advantage of his gullibility.

Thrusting a twenty-pound note into his hand she said 'Hi, Barnaby, may I have a word?' She explained that people were taking advantage of his good nature just so they could mock him. 'The pound coin is smaller but it's worth twice as much as the fifty pence piece' she explained, and you could have had a brand-new bicycle, too' she added sympathetically 'bicycles can't remember their way around, Barnaby.'

'Oh, arrh, I knows that ma'am' said Barnaby with a happy grin, 'folks do like to laugh at I, but it ain't all bad being the village idiot. Take the young widow Jenkins, now. She invites me to tea three times a week and everyone in the village thinks she's a good soul for taking pity on me. But she fucks me every time 'cos she likes my big willie.' He smiled broadly. 'I never tells anyone so she thinks I can't remember, see?'

'Oh, I see,' said the embarrassed tourist, blushing to her roots.

'And another thing, ma'am, the tourists would soon stop giving me money if I took the pound every time, wouldn't they?'

'Ah, I understand now' said the lady, smiling warmly, 'thank you, Barnaby, I feel much better for knowing that.'

She was making her way back to the tour bus when Sligh, guiding duties done, passed by on the other side of the street.'

'Hi, dad' called Barnaby 'how did we do this morning? I just got another twenty quid.'

The shocked tourist turned around looking open-mouthed at Barnaby.

He grinned at her 'There'll be another group o' you daft buggers coming this afternoon' he said 'T'aint Oi that's gullible Missus.'

Sweet and Sour

Short Shorts

As part of an exercise in conciseness, I write a snippet most weeks using exactly fifty words.

House Clearance

Gus Guller, surveying the possessions of the late Mrs Burford, spotted the genuine Lowery painting. 'A worthless copy' he told her naïve nephew, 'I'll give you £5 for the frame.'

He went upstairs inspecting.

Gus returned; the nephew handed him the frame.

'Where's the picture?'

'Back garden, on the bonfire.'

Crab Paste

The wife went to pick up the prescriptions yesterday. 'Bring me something for a sandwich,' I told her.

Back home, she made me a sandwich. I took one bite and spit it out 'Good God woman, what's this?'

'Crabs paste' she said, 'it was on special offer at the chemists.'

A Word of Warning

I saw grumpy old Fred approaching, I can't stand him, so I crossed the road.

He saw me avoiding him. 'Dog' he yelled, his brolly pointing.

'Pig' I screamed back at him, brandishing my walking stick.

That was the moment before a Rottweiler sank its fangs into my arse.

Raising Cane

"I will not tolerate violence" our headmaster roared, thumping his desk. He gave Billy and me six of the best.

"So much for non-violence" I muttered. I got two more strokes.

Billy and I had fought over Polly Perks; she promptly rejected us both.

Ah, well, another lesson learned.

The Wigan Treasure Hunt

Participants were handed a clue sheet: "Look for a rook on a dock". Everybody dashed to Wigan Pier.

'Found it old George said, pointing to a small statue.

'That's a duck on a rock,' said his Missus.

'Look at the clue setter's name.' said George.

'WA Spooner? Oh, Clever you.'

Modern Marriage

Our twenty-year-old daughter came home all excited last night. 'Mummy, Daddy' she said, 'I'm getting married, I'm so happy.'

Her mother said 'Oh, that's lovely,' tell me how it happened.'

'John took me to dinner, then we had sex at his place, then asked me to be his first wife.'

Care Home Dating

'Old Albert asked me for a date, Edna. What was he like with you?'

'A gentleman, Doris. Ritz hotel, champagne, lobster, the works. Then afterwards he tore apart my new silk knickers and ravaged me all night.'

'Oh, so I shouldn't go then?'

'You go dear, just wear old knickers.'

If you have enjoyed at least some of these stories I am pleased. I have more work on:

Sweet and Sour

Trigger warning: All contain references to sex and violence.

The Negotiator
1976: Arms and explosives are flooding into Northern Ireland from an unknown source. Innocent people are being butchered on the streets. Action must be taken.
An undercover mission to find the source of the arms is given to one man. He is drawn against his will on a harrowing journey to Eire, the USA and Libya, his life is hourly hanging in the balance. A tale of spying and dying.

https://www.amazon.co.uk/dp/B07BD4YX72

When Terror Strikes
A ruthless drug baron is funding a terrorist cell hell-bent on turning the streets of London into rivers of blood. A dead teenager and a man determined to bring her killers to justice. A wall of silence surrounds her death. Jack Ellis, a retired intelligence officer, is determined to break that silence by doing whatever it takes. Bent cops, treachery in high places, and a murderous gang stand in his way. Drastic action is called for.

https://www.amazon.co.uk/dp/B0787MNBJ3

The Brat

A young girl is running across desolate moorland at night being pursued by ruthless killers. She knows too much.

She is rescued by an over-the-hill ex-mercenary with PTSD and a bad attitude. He knows nothing about kids and doesn't want to but cannot bring himself to abandon her.

The girl shares her secret with him. Now the Russian mafia needs them both dead.

Fast paced and realistic, a page turner

   https://www.amazon.co.uk/dp/B086DQ12WP

The Pendulum Swings

Two murders twenty years apart in a small village. A young artist and his new love get drawn into the mystery by a strange caller. Someone close has a guilty secret to hide and is prepared to kill to keep it. Can the ancient art of dowsing help before the killer strikes again? An intriguing whodunnit.

   https://www.amazon.co.uk/dp/B0855KY7MF

A Sting in the Tale

This is an eclectic collection of punchy short stories, sometimes romantic, often with a devious twist. It is your ideal companion for a long journey, or to while away odd moments of your spare time. An ideal inexpensive present.

   https://www.amazon.co.uk/dp/B07FTVYMWQ

Sweet and Sour

The author can be contacted
ppap.writeme@gmail.com

Blocat publication Oldham UK All rights reserved

Printed in Great Britain
by Amazon